MARS AND THE LOST PLANET MAN

The unauthorized history of the solar system

MARS AND THE LOST PLANET MAN

A NOVEL

LOU BALDIN

Contents of this book acquired through personal experiences with beings, not of Earth.

MARS AND THE LOST PLANET MAN

TABLE OF CONTENTS

PROLOGUE 15

RENEGADES 21

SAM 24

EONS PAST 32

WAR OF THE PLANETS......................................42

MARTIANS...54

BIGFOOT...72

PLANET MAN...81

DESTRUCTION OF PLANET MAN 115

HUMAN ABDUCTIONS.......................................131

MUMMIES...138

LARGE WINGED BEINGS...................................144

MARS BEFORE THE LAST WAR.........................151

POLTERGEIST...160

REPTILIANS..167

GODS OF THE STAR SYSTEM 173

HADES...193

INNER EARTH...200

SOLAR BEINGS...203

MANIFESTING DESIRES.....................................207

BOOKS BY THE AUTHOR..211

Sanity is the prevailing level of psychosis in a society at any given time

Lou Baldin

PROLOGUE

The universe is a vast playground that is maintained by a collaboration of highly spiritualized beings. Such beings, rarely, if ever manifest onto the playground that they oversee. The universe is but one of many endless physical and nonphysical universes in existence. Universes in general, are in the category of perpetuity, never beginning or ending, and infinite.

Universes are and exist inside of endless dimensions. Dimensions are infinite, never-ending, perpetual and relatively bizarre.

Infinity is a concept and reality near impossible to articulate and comprehend while trapped and confined inside of three-dimensional illusions. The human mind has access to higher and lower dimensions but is handicapped by the fixation and the absurdity of illusionary reality.

That handicap allows humans to believe they originated by accident of nature on this one planet. A planet which happens to be in the "sweet zone" (habitable zone), around the star (sun).

Such illusions make it difficult to grasp a far different reality concerning this star system and the billions of life-sustaining star systems within most galaxies in the universe.

All planets in a star system are in a "habitable zone" of some sort (habitable and unique to each planet and planetary system, and the beings and creatures existing on them).

Intelligent life in the cosmos remains a taboo subject for most people on Earth (less so now as more people of the world wake up to realities made possible through technological advancements in astronomy).

Believing that life exists somewhere in the universe other than on Earth and that such life has the wherewithal to make the trip to Earth, is where most people draw the line.

Regardless of what most people think or believe, life is abundant all over the universe, in the endless billions of galaxies, and the star systems inside of galaxies. Humans, for the most part, remain unaware of galactic marvels and the prevalent travel by industrious higher beings residing in a thriving and vibrant universe.

Taboos helped cement and propagate institutionalized illusions postured by religious and scientific establishments (that are often in collaboration).

Religious and scientific institutions have cooperated for the reason of feeding the concept of planetary sovereignty to the masses of humanity. Delusions have kept extraterrestrial reality in the science fiction "bin" for countless generations.

Planetary sovereignty, as suggested in Darwin's theory of evolution, is a farce. The origins of man, beast, insects and vegetation are extraterrestrial and by purposeful design.

Nothing originated on planet Earth, no flora, fauna, or any of the minerals and elements that make up the building blocks of the so-called physical world. Essence and physical existence come to Earth off-the-shelf, fully developed and ready to go. Plant and animal modifications, happens, with external determination to the living things brought here from elsewhere in the galaxy, and are made to adapt to local conditions on this planet by extraterrestrial technicians and their nonhuman and human cohorts.

Humans experience a physical existence but are not physical beings. Not even while in the perceived physical flesh.

Under a microscope, what we call physical, the elements that make up flesh and blood, are not physical at all. Everything we see, taste, touch, smell and hear is illusionary sensations, created by massless vibrations birthed by mass from the star. The same mass that gives life to creations brought here from beings originating from other star systems, who are saddled with a propagation gene, and on a mission.

What humans perceive as reality is but a mysterious electrical element that behaves in a bizarre and humanly inexplicable manner, concerning known particle physics.

Scientists studying sub-particle phenomena are bewildered by the antics they see in the subatomic world. No less than the star gazers (astrophysicists), and NASA, who also see things in the cosmic realms that they can't explain or understand. Such institutions of knowledge have no inclination of ever enlightening the human masses any more than their fellow scientists in the quantum mechanics department. The enigma that is "enlightenment" comes from the enlightened, not from mortal religious schemes and scientific suppositions.

Most things are made of mysterious quantum particles. Particles that project into our relative human three-dimensional reality (human reality). Subatomic particles reside in the paranormal and ethereal realms, the realms that are often laughed at when brought up in casual conversations or in scientific circles among serious-looking scientists. Likewise, in the outer world, where the stars rule over the night skies, and extraterrestrial creatures and beings mingle freely with humans in a paranormal haze (the three-dimensional reality humans are pickled inside of).

RENEGADES

Sinister beings "infest" star systems located in the outer reaches of the Milky Way galaxy, where Earth resides. Such beings were discarded, expelled from vast stretches of star systems and were left to linger in the dark reaches of space that exists between star systems. Some of those beings made their way to other star systems and managed to penetrate defenses that most star systems have in place to keep intruders out.

Some star systems are more porous and consequently more attractive to renegades than other star systems. And thus, fail to prevent many renegade beings from entering. Numerous renegade races are destroyed by the "gods" before they enter star systems, and much more are captured and or destroyed after they penetrate the star system.

Once inside the fences of star systems, the most tenacious of renegades often manage to find their way into planetary systems and burrow into and below the surfaces of moons and planets. No moon or planet in this star system is free of renegade infestation. Some renegade clans go dormant soon after they find hiding places and remain inactive sometimes for centuries to avoid detection by the gods, and other overlords who rule the star system.

Local gods employ and make use of some renegade tribes, using them for their own purposes and providing renegades with limited privileges and rewards in exchange for services rendered. Such transactions are common in the galaxy and are part of the goings-on in the billions of star systems incorporated inside of galaxies.

SAM

I watched eight-foot-tall winged beings build cities out of solid blocks of granite, with relative ease. Beings and machines quarried blocks of stone to exact measurements, with tools that emerged from the beings and etched and carved the blocks flawlessly.

The beings operated in concert alongside mechanized creatures in a symphony. Surveying, excavating and setting large stones in place as consistent as if they were working on an assembly line. Beings and machines worked at speeds that blurred their movements, making them nearly invisible to the unaided human eye. Completed Structures seemingly appeared out of thin air, magically, manifesting in front of me, like the instant formation of ice crystals on a snowflake.

It was a spectacle that was shown to me, on a room size display, which was on board a ship (UFO) that was hidden in the clouds above my house, during a stormy night. The room was a type of holographic environment that created the appearance of being at the actual site (wherever that might have been, I wasn't told).

From that race of beings came one that escorted me on an extraordinary journey to explore the star system and revealed some of its mystery and histories. I called the creature, Sam.

Sam displayed male and female characteristics and exhibited delicate and not so subtle paranormal qualities. Sam had strange physical and supernatural features that manifested in perplexingly indescribable ways, and some that are impossible to recount.

My reasonable recollection and description of a portion of what Sam showed me, and told me, follows.

Sam had wings like those of a seraph but claimed not to be one. Sam's wings did not flap as do the wings of a bird or used the aerodynamics of lift as do the wings of an airplane. Sam's wings were stationary and functioned stealthily, delivering and providing a peculiar and exhilarating mode of travel to me. Sam was able to cloak, and I became invisible when Sam did. Sam departed from the ship we were in, and I literally traveled on Sam's back, as if I were riding a large bird. The bizarre ordeal seemed normal and natural to me at the time.

There was never a feeling that I would fall off of Sam. I was somehow secured on Sam's back as if I was in a cockpit of a fighter jet. Sam might have been a machine, yet Sam communicated with me as if he, she or it, were intelligent, aware and human (Sam was anything but human).

Sam transported me to a large cavern deep inside of Earth and showed me a civilization of strange beings that loitered on the streets below us. The humanoid beings shuffled around on dark streets with no apparent destination. The place had a Dark Age, medieval appearance to it. Yet, I saw no animals, horses, dogs, hogs, chickens or any creatures that are typically associated with medieval places and villages.

People milled about in drab dress and with forlorn facial expressions. People walked on the sidewalks in front of rows of stone buildings, some that had been carved into the cave walls, or strolled along the winding corridors and streets.

Many other structures were freestanding and stood alone, as monoliths and away from the center of the town. Low-lying attached buildings with street-level shops and apartments above them made up the majority of structures in the town.

The town appeared large but was short on vitality. It covered a massive section of the cavern, which seemed to have no end to it. Buildings and streets lacked cohesiveness. No geometrical layout, everything was randomly built, and the town and its people, were equally and extremely characterless.

The residents looked to be overwhelmingly humanoid "people" that were larger than humans but wingless and smaller than Sam was. Other creatures (beings) in the town, were much smaller, humanoid types, with various deformities.

Sam never landed in the town or walked on the streets when I was with her. He hovered above the streets and the peculiar looking buildings dotting the cavern floor and over the peculiar people that ambled below us. The people were aware of Sam and me and seemed indifferent to our intrusion into their town.

The cavern had numerous underground passages, bridges, and tunnels that were cut into or through the solid rock. Sam entered one of the tunnels and after traveling for a time emerged into an area that had a multifaceted labyrinth inside of it. The place was foreboding, and it was a place impossible to navigate without the ability of flight (according to Sam).

Sam had no difficulty navigating the endless miles of the barbaric labyrinth, and stretching as far as my human eyes could see.

Dark and hostile in appearance, the labyrinth was lined with menacing iron spikes and razor-sharp shards of multicolored crystals jutting every which way. The labyrinth was designed to devour flesh, and no less, the mind and spirit. The labyrinth was lifeless, with no signs of man or beast stirring inside of the ominous web.

Sam came to a stop in a large room inside one of the hundreds of cubes that were woven into a system of grids, each suspended above a dark and deep hole, somewhere inside the labyrinth.

Sam then opened up like an exotic flower in bloom and expelled an object from her mouth that morphed into a glowing multicolored, multifaceted cube/orb, pervasively changing its shape and color. A vision of a book emerged from the orb and pages from it overflowed with a mysterious material. The material flowed into my mind, and I could see things that had transpired in parts of the star system over periods of millions of years. Overcome by the massive amount of information that swarmed into my head, I lost consciousness.

Revived, I found myself back inside the ship. Sam had vanished, and I was returned to my suburban home by a Serpent being. The Serpent was humanoid, with a scaly face, as that of a snake but with definite human features and characteristics. Shorter than I, the Serpent had two arms, two legs and a trim and fit body. I didn't see its backside, so I don't know if it had a tail (as some of the scaly reptilian beings that I had encountered previously had).

The Serpent had a mouth but communicated telepathically with me. I was unsure of the gender of the Serpent, or if it had a gender. I didn't ask, and it never said. The Serpent was kind and cordial. The Serpent reiterated what was in the book at a rapid rate of speed which made little sense to my conscious human mind. The Serpent told me that I would remember what I needed to remember and to do whatever I wished to do with that material. I was told by the Serpent that the material had more than informational qualities to it, and left it ambiguous.

The Serpent moved speedily around me and changed places frequently, moving from one side of me to the other side, then behind me and back in front of me. Stopping each time, only momentarily, long enough so that I could snatch a glimpse of the strange creature buzzing around me. It couldn't or wouldn't remain still, or stop so that I could ask it questions.

But it communicated with me while it phased in and out of my line of sight.

The Serpent touched me and it stopped moving, and the room became a blur. I was now moving at the same vibration level as the Serpent, and we moved throughout the house at lightning speeds. No one was home, and we moved outside the house and entered a neighbor's house. The neighbors were home but didn't see us or know that anyone was in their home, watching them. The Serpent slowed down a bit, and I could see the neighbors clearly. They did not see or sense the Serpent or me. The Serpent returned me to my house and then vanished. Leaving me without further explanation of why it invaded the neighbor's home, with me in tow.

I came from a Catholic background and wondered if the Serpent was a demon (as in the Garden of Eden, with Adam and Eve). The Serpent was not visible to me and answered telepathically that it was not a demon. "But how could I know," I responded in my mind. I was told it was not for me to know, or for any human to know the true nature of the spirit world.

Information imparted to me by the Serpent:

EONS PAST

The five inner planets of the star system (solar system), Mercury, Venus, Earth, Mars, and Man, were populated by physical and nonphysical beings that resided at the lower end of the galactic spiritual spectrum. Other planets exist in the inner region but remain elusive and transient, without a fixed orbit around the star (sun), or the mass that would perturb the orbits of the planets and moons within the star system. Information about those types of planets is inadequate for a comprehensive explanation of them (except for a smidgeon of details dripped in the next chapter of this book).

The outer planets, those near the edge of obscurity and their oppressive distances from Earth, also entertained and hosted lower level beings for a variety of reasons and purposes. Purposes that suited galactic overseers (the cadre of beings calling the shots on billions of star systems within galaxies).

Such overseers are not gods but are above the gods, the gods that menace and shepherd the creatures and beings within their jurisdictions and domains (star systems such as the one we humans call home).

Gods are the beings that operate at the highest levels within each star system in the galaxy. The gods control and enable various conflicts between competing clans, societies and races of beings residing within each star system.

Star systems in the Milky Way, have subordinate administrators (gods) that rule mostly behind the scenes and unbeknownst to the lower beings (humans and other similar types of beings). Many non-human type beings existing on the surface and in the interiors of planets, moons, asteroids, comets and the artificial and untethered planets, know a thing or two about the gods. What anyone breed of beings knows about the gods depends on their level of awareness of the cosmic goings-on in the universe.

Dominant and once dominant races of beings in this star system are the Serpents, Martians, and several other types of Reptilians (besides the Serpents), and the Humans from planet Man. Less dominant races are Earth humans, and a smattering of indigenous and nonindigenous creatures that have collected on and inside of planets, moons and interstellar debris (asteroids and comets); and the creatures that remain out of sight and out of mind (of humans, mostly) and are from the various nonindigenous Renegade races, with the makings of human roots.

Some of the various and peculiar life forms (creatures) in the star system, existed for short durations and quickly evaporate away like morning dew, after their (unknown) reason for being ended.

Other types of mysterious and whimsical life forms are in a constant state of change (morphing), in their ever persevering attempts to penetrate barriers put into place by the gods. The gods endeavor to keep infectious critters out of the star system and out of the planets and moons within the star system.

Star defensive systems are constantly changing (upgrading) thousands of times a second in order to repel the myriad of contagious and intrusive (mysterious creatures, beings, and their entourage of bizarre residues) from entering the planetary system. A smattering of such intergalactic contagions succeeds in manifesting and morphing to the conditions necessary to penetrate star systems fortifications. Once in, the beings and creatures subtly pervade and interacted with indigenous beings, plants, and animal life, on a number of planets and moons.

To counteract cosmic biotic infestations that exist in the cold darkness of space, the gods implement drones (biting insects) to monitor and control invading species of viruses and plagues, with viruses and plagues designed by the gods to specifically consume and destroy toxic invaders. Occasionally, such countermeasures end up wiping out entire communities, cities and whole populations of various beings and creatures (humans or otherwise) infected by the intergalactic viruses, bugs, germs, and diseases.

Like common house flies, existing only to deposit maggots into carrion, in order to dispose of dead flesh, some creatures looked for and looked after the carcasses of human souls. The dead (living dead), souls temporarily housed inside of the human or other types of hybrid creatures and containers, left to resolve themselves in a future time and place. Such incarcerated souls lingered alongside other humans, living semi-normal lives and interacting but had little if any purpose in their own existence, other than to get through their current life, whatever the experience.

Other categories of non-native beings circulating in and around star systems, in general, were of the Renegade clans. Beings that were deposed, exiled, cast off, from home planets on alien and distant star systems, and allowed by galactic overseers to mingle overly and covertly with indigenous races, within designated star systems in the Milky Way.

Sam communicated telepathically and interjected additional information into the material from that which flowed from the orb and the Serpent. Offering me supplementary perspectives on the most bizarre of life forms in order for me to grasp bits of the supernatural happenings prevalent in the star system.

Sam or the Serpent or Sam the Serpent, continued to be with me in a place inside of the interstellar ship, where information was transmitted, fed to me, in three-dimensional derisive verbiages (like Rodney Dangerfield, I got no respect).

I was shown phenomena that intruded into the strata of differing time periods and eras encompassing this star system, while Sam and I journeyed inside of a paranormal, astronomical, 3d-mind-blowing, space vessel.

I was taken to a forbidden and mysterious planet hidden within the star system and inhabited by magical and mysterious beings and creatures (no magic mushrooms). Such planets were not made of the same material (matter) that makes up the known planets and moons in this star system. It had no gravity, oceans or sky. The land was whimsical and quirky as were the beings in existence on it (no DMT or other types of hallucinogenic material). Sam and I were motionless and inside of, and enveloped by, a large gyrating orb that provided an extraordinary view of the goings on all around us.

The orb became momentarily stationary, and we could see flurries of delicate creatures of various sizes and colors flow by as if schools of fish, within a massive waterless ocean. Some creatures were winged, and sported fairy qualities, fluttering and darting and some stopped and looked at me with equal curiosity as I had of them (no wine, liquor or beer). I was inside a cosmic fishbowl and looking out onto the strange and unknowable creatures living outside of the fish bowl.

Sam told me that such mysterious beings collected on planets and made themselves known (on some level or not at all) to the indigenous peoples in the regions they visited or invaded. On earth, some such beings are referred to as fairies, elves, gremlins and any number of mythical and paranormal creatures. They were a mess of various types of sprites that affected, plagued or interact with selected humans (people gifted to see and occasionally interact and communicate with the mystical beings, and or be tormented by them).

The bizarre planet turned and spun every which way as if it were trying to rid itself of my presence. The orb, Sam and I were inside of, irritated the planet as if the orb were an invasive species, an insect, as a flea on a dog. Sam said that eventually it, the planet, would penetrate the orb and destroy its contents (me). Sam assured me that we would depart the planet before that happened. The size of the planet was impossible to detect since we could not orbit the planet and see if from space (and Sam didn't tell me the size). The planet could only be viewed from the inside of it or on it. Any foreign object, like myself, was unwelcomed and could only be there for a short duration, with the aid of Sam, the perpetually morphing, Serpent being.

We stayed on the planet long enough for Sam to speak information to me without the danger of other beings capturing and destroying or distorting the information.

Serpents and the gods of the star system were the two races that had limited abilities to enter into the bizarre planets like the one we were on. All other creatures and beings in the star system lacked the capabilities to find such planets, and no ability to enter the planets if they did manage to find them. Foreign beings and creatures without the proper escort were absorbed into the planet, captured, expelled or destroyed. The planets and Sam said there were many of them in this star system, gave up limited information to the Serpents and gods, and little or none to other lesser beings (mortals), in the category of humans and Martians.

I was not on that planet to gather information on the planet, I was brought there to receive information about the rest of the star system, and only a fraction I received, and far less I retained.

WAR OF THE PLANETS

During an earlier epoch in this star system (millions of years before modern humans inhabited earth), Serpents controlled Mercury and Venus; Martians controlled Mars (believe they did), as was true for humans that believed they controlled planet Man (the destroyed planetary system now known as the asteroid belt).

Allowed and sometimes encouraged by star system leaders (the gods), Renegades infiltrated, manipulated, and influenced governing bodies, clans, and tribes of Martians (on Mars) for a duration of hundreds of millions of Earth years. Renegades attempted to infiltrate Human populations on planet Man, but the gods shielded the humans from most renegade influences and tampering.

(Due to the numerous unique time zones within the star system, Earth years is used.)

Before the rift (battles that broke out between the inner planets), millions of years in the past, Martians battled primarily with the Serpent races. Martians dispatched fleets of ships to planets Venus and Mercury, with the intent of destroying the

Serpent race, and remove themselves from the yoke of Serpent meddling in Martian affairs.

Serpents had previously subjugated Earth and placed administrators into the governing body of Earth, and its moons (earth had two moons during that era). Soon after subduing Earth, Serpents installed outposts on planet Man, and on all of Man's numerous territories in the star system.

Planet Man and its extensive network of subsidiaries (outposts) were under siege by Serpents and Martians. Both Serpents and Martians maintained outposts on planet Man. But Martians remained isolated from humans and were never allowed to intermix physically or socially, by the gods, who forbade it (it happened anyway). The Serpents had designs on taking over planet Man, and the other inner planets, Venus, Mercury, Earth and their territories, which were located on numerous planetoids and space cities.

Planet Man was passive and neutral, and in a defensive posture prior to its demise. Planet Man was not equipped to launch a counter attack against antagonists that were flirting to take over the planet, and its many dominions scattered all over the star system.

Martians shied away from open warfare with the Serpents on Earth. Serpents had impenetrable fleets of warships orbiting Earth and Earth's moons. Martians did maintain covert operations on Earth, many, and employed hybrids and animals in subversive plots that sowed seeds for future deployments with the intentions of eventually invading Earth (pre-human era).

One of Earth's moons, the smaller of the two, was used against Earth by the Serpents. Serpents exploded the moon causing it to shatter and fall onto Earth's surface, over an extended period of time. Fragments from the destroyed moon bombarded earth with meteor showers that lasted thousands of years and started an era of destruction over the existing animal and plant life, which culminated in the sterilization of the planet Earth. It was a planned process to cleanse the earth of the infestations, primarily from Mars and Venus. Other lesser invasions from outer planet insurgents and their contaminants, including the mysterious and deceptively belligerent Renegade races, were also decimated.

Dinosaurs and other creatures were placed on Earth for the amusement of the human populations of Man (and numerous other beings with access to Earth). Earth was a zoo and was visited by billions of humans from planet Man, for millions of years.

Earth was a destination point mainly for entertainment but had other nefarious uses as well. Earth was a neutral planet not belonging to any of the dominant races in the star system, during that era. Earth was also a place of barbaric training and ritualized killing, by renegade clans. Those and other despicable activities by rebel beings culminated in perverse indulgences that turned Earth into a blood-fest-planet. Such activities lasted for countless millennia and poisoned the planet (similar events in a reduced form continue to this day). Renegade races from Venus and distant star systems relentlessly competed and battled against each other and other inhabitants of Earth.

Battles intended to feed an insatiable desire for blood and gore, pervaded, and were fed by numerous beings and races that took up residence on Earth, for the exclusive aim to join in on the barbarous sport. Taking prisoners became the end game and motivation to add to the ritualized tortures and killings in order to appease, and for the pleasure, of renegade demigods, that had erected stone settlements on Earth.

Temples were built, and prisoners were taken to them and sacrificed alive to horrendous Jurassic-era beasts and creatures. The beasts were fed ahead of time so that they would toy with the victims before tearing into them, prolonging the horror of the kill, for hours and sometimes days, for the sadistic pleasure of the spectators.

Ritualized killings of humans (after the fall of planet Man), Martians and others, culminated in feasts and activities, where single events continued for weeks, months and sometimes for years. Cannibalism and the eating of desecrated flesh accompanied the festivals. Frenzies often erupted, and spectators turned on each other climaxing into orgies of bloodlust, and the eventual horrific death for most of the participants, and portions of the audience.

After a time, Renegades began breeding humanoids to feed their unquenchable need for barbaric pleasures, and the depraved hunger for flesh and gore. The humanoids had no souls, for the Renegades had no means of procuring souls for the bodies they created. But the humanoid creatures did have an element of Renegade soul that passed on from and existed in their spawn. The gods destroyed some of the renegade civilizations when they were discovered, or when the cries from tormented flesh became repulsively loud and nauseating.

Often, gods would kill or dispose of the Renegade tribes, and salvage the humanoid societies created by the Renegades. But only for those creatures that the gods deemed had some ecological worth for planet Earth. Gods ruled over the selected, salvaged masses, and taught them rudimentary skills of survival before turning them loose to endure/survive on their own.

Once left alone, renegade spawned-societies, were subjected to conscription by any and all rogue groups that conquered and enslaved the vulnerable villages and people. Humans and other branches of prehuman linages (Renegade spawn) faced constant peril and were preyed upon by various Renegade clans and other creatures, which were always on the lookout for new or additional victims for their ritualized games.

This star system was not all war and gore but enough so that it attracted infinite types of beings that craved to enslave lesser beings and place them into their own societies as servants, labor, and cannon fodder, for battles against other beings and creatures. The gods permitted the calamity brought on by the Renegades, to persist and flourish for a time. The gods allowed plenty of room for a free-for-all between renegade clans, as part of the ecological process. It was a type of food chain that maintained an order of things, with the top predators keeping the lesser prey, in check, on their toes and on their knees. Renegades battled and killed each other off, which also served a purpose for the gods.

Maggots feast on the flesh and leave the bones. Otherwise, the stench of rotting carcasses would desecrate the land (an allegory about renegade effect). Over millennium, the bones of multitudes of beings that had found their way to Earth, and then fell victim to other beings on Earth, added the useful rudimentary product to the planet.

Dinosaurs did their part to cleanse the Earth of previous civilizations. The lengthy Jurassic period added ecological prospects for future developments and the societies destined to inhabit Earth, millions of years after the Jurassic era. Dinosaurs were used for the purpose of capturing and consuming many types of renegade beings that had alluded capture by other means, and who were often disguised as species of dinosaurs themselves. Renegades created hybrids, a mixture of themselves mixed with various breeds of dinosaurs, and other types of animals and aggressive beasts.

Ferocious creatures competed for food and domination over lesser creatures, including an early version of humans (by Reptilian design). Human souls and the essences of other higher and lower beings were able to enter dinosaurs and similar creatures to experience savagery against the souls that were attached, strapped-in, inside of prey.

Barbaric experiences (predator and prey) were masochistic games, popular and widespread, activities propagated by lower level beings, and often voluntary. Beings placed into prey for the contemptible need of satisfying bloodcurdling lust. Blood-lust on many levels dominated activities in the Jurassic era.

After the destruction of planet Man, Earth received a new commission, where much of the animal and plant life was destroyed or removed, in preparation for a renewed use of Earth. Earth required a shuffling of residents, so as to adhere to a diverse human population that was to be placed on the planet in stages. Several resident races were removed, relocated or eliminated (slaughtered) to make way for anthropoids and other types of humanoids.

Selected renegade races were infused into the stock of Martians and the humans from Man, which created subdivisions that would become elements of lineages (ancestors), the forebears of the current human races. A humanoid mixture (design) that carried special genes for the types of souls destined to live within unique human containers.

Sectors of this star system were lawless during extended and drawn out periods, post planet Man. Portions of the star system were literally abandoned for a time as part of the cleansing operation imposed periodically by powers in the galactic guard (rulers above the local gods). Planets were allowed to rest and ferment for lengthy periods between soul-culturing-epochs.

Dead or dying souls made up a substantial portion of souls marooned (isolated) on Earth for millions of years, before, during, and after the age of large and bizarre animals, such as dinosaurs.

During the times that star systems underwent restructuring they became havens for renegade influxes, like flies to a carcass (allowed by the powers in charge). Renegades were herded and funneled from nearby star systems (mostly from the darkness between star systems, where they had fled to hide) by enforcers, as part of the fermentation and cleansing process on selected planetary systems.

Renegades were exiled beings and hungry for conditional power and a semblance of autonomy (freedoms and privileges that they had lost on their own planets and would never regain). Renegades were eager and willing mercenaries, and acting like vultures and maggots, allowed to ravage and rape populations on forsaken planets, moons and space cities, whose corruption enticed them to rapid fermentation and expansion.

A few Renegades yearned to return to their place of origin. To the stars sparkling in the night sky like beacons calling them home. Repentant beings have made and continue to make attempts to regain former glory with restitutions, appeasements, and conciliatory gestures to the consulate beings from their home regions.

Consulates with the power to grant amnesty, and representing star systems that have active citizens and citizens that have been banished, occasionally make diplomatic rounds to this star system and other star systems in the region.

Most Renegades are unsuccessful in their attempts to obtain pardons, their pleas falling on diplomatic deaf ears. But a few resilient, determined and remorseful types, do manage to find a way back to their former intergalactic abodes.

Immortals (soul-bearing beings) have an eternity to resolve problems, and some know it, those that know not, haven't enough soul left to know anything.

MARTIANS

Martians were outnumbered and outgunned and lacked the technological wherewithal for survival during the volatile period. Martian wars against the Serpents lasted countless eons and sputtered out ages ago. Martian refugees were exiled to Earth by the Serpents, with the most recent batch, prior to the human Renaissance era, on Earth.

Martians were a much more powerful race in the past, and they were able to hold their own against the Serpents, and other races, for millions of years before their eventual downfall. Mars retains a significant and diverse population to this day. However, it is wildly scattered throughout the star system.

Hidden on the surface and deep within Mar's innards, are the remnants of a once dominant Martian civilization. Martians continue to occupy near and distant orbits around Mars, on spacefaring vessels (for a quick getaway). Martians remain subservient to various Reptilian races, which includes the Serpents. Serpents control Martian movements and habitation in the star system, as they do for humans, as well.

Present day humans are unaware or vaguely aware of Martian life, and the extent of life throughout the star system (which most humans are in denial of). Populations of various creatures and beings on planets, moons and the billions of space cities (ships), although decreased significantly from past millennia, remains robust in this system. As is true with infants who are unaware of the hustle and bustle and goings-on in the world around them, humans on Earth, are unaware of the goings on in the star system all around them.

Before the downfall of Mars, Martians battled Serpents relentlessly for control over planet Man and its four moons. Over the centuries, Mars made significant inroads into Man, spreading their own breeds secretly on that doomed planetary system. Martians were able to remain hidden from the humans on Man and avoided detection by the Serpents (so they believed). Serpents were always aware of Martian intentions for planet Man, and the Martian penetration of that planet.

Planet Man was dominated by a pure breed and a solitary race of humans. Humans remained mostly untainted for the greater part of Man's multimillion year existence. But fringe beings including Martians managed to hide within planet Man and its four moons. Mysteriously, Serpents and the gods permitted the worms in the apple of Man.

Nevertheless, Serpents had no intentions of allowing the Martians to gain a permanent hold on planet Man. But knowing that the planet was destined for destruction, the Serpents bided their time, and patience, with the Martians, and other infestations on Man.

Planet Man had the largest human population in the star system. One that was spread out on other planets, moons and the thousands of space cities that were incorporated inside of massive starships.

Man's extensive network of outposts, connected every segment of the star system together like that of a spider's web. Humans from Man collaborated with various other entities and races throughout the star system, providing services and trading goods with all the planets and moons in the system.

Humans, above all the other beings in the star system, were trusted (and manipulated) by all. Nevertheless, the humans were protected, for the most part, by the gods. That protection came to an end after millions of years, when the gods forsook the humans of Man, for a greater interstellar purpose (demands from higher beings that were above the gods, and residing in the cosmic realms).

Serpents were chosen by the gods to pull the plug on the pure-breed humans on Man, its moons, and the whole of the human network across the star system. One of the reasons (but not the most important of reasons) that humans faced annihilation, along with their extensive network that connected all the beings, and the various races on planets and moons, had to do with a parasitic Reptilian strain of beings, which had leached on to the humans for their near perfect genomic biological structure. It was an ironic paradox because the Reptilian race was permitted to do what they did by higher echelon galactic rulers, for millions of years.

Cleansing and keeping it untainted (the human genetic material), inherent in humans of Man, was past its prime, and no longer paramount to the Serpents, who had been instructed on the future plans for humans on Earth. In the aftermath of the reform in the star system, a pure breed of human was no longer the objective or desire of the overseers of that particular branch of humanity (the humans of Man).

Post-destruction of Man, and two of its moons, Serpents directed their wrath on Mars. Sparing the planet but killing off large parcels of Human/Martian hybrids, which were inhabitants of Mars. Before the destruction of Man, a number of Humans had been taken to Mars by Martians and were bred with other beings including Martians, to create a diverse Martian race that had human attributes.

Martians intended to use the Human/Martian hybrids to create and expand Martian colonies on Earth. A few colonies and outpost were created by Martians but eventually they too were rooted out and exterminated by the Serpents.

Serpents enslaved the Martians that had survived the brutal attack on Mars, and most of its space colonies. An assault that simultaneously destroyed every Martian city on the planet and most of the Martian colonies off the planet, in a single blow.

Earth experienced a similar cleansing, and restructuring, to make way for a portion of the surviving humans from planet Man (spared by the gods for the reason of seeding and sowing the Earth). Humans were stored in large container ships as big as a medium-sized moon, and released in batches, periodically, onto earth and other regions (planets, moons, space cities) within the star system.

Star system overseers (the gods) did little to interfere in the squabbles between renegade clans (which were many). Instead, they encouraged and sanctioned processes that engaged renegades against each other, stirring the pot that affected the affairs of humans and other races on Earth. It was a recipe concocted by the Serpents, and approved by the gods, to hasten the decimation of existing races in order to pave the way for new and diverse breeds of humans.

Humanoid species of beings replaced the spiritually depleted beings and creatures that roamed on Earth for eons, and whose endless billions of carcasses, over the centuries, fertilized the soil of Earth, millions of years prior to the entry of humanoids.

Human type containers (humanoid bodies) were used to store souls from various star systems in the Milky Way, for a multitude of reasons, including extensive incarceration and psychological manipulation. Like a seed bank, various types of souls were collected from far off star systems and crossbred in the furnaces of surrogate star systems, by spiritualized beings. Where souls resided and flourished in the bodies of humanoids and other types of containers, on the planetary bodies of that star system.

Serpents were commissioned by the overseers (gods) and received approval and privileges to establish kingdoms and population centers on Earth. Earth was destined to receive a series of races from various star systems in the galaxy but also from Mars and Venus (Serpents called Venus, home). Races from other star systems were crossbred with Martians, Venusians, and humans, and make up the primary races that are only the traces of the ancestors of modern humans.

Multiple races were kept inside of container-ships (spaceships) in orbit around Earth. Bodies, and sometimes with souls inside of them, were/are suspended in a soup of mysterious fluids until reanimated and dispersed, periodically, onto planets. Vikings (from Mars) are one of the most recent concoctions that were dropped off on Earth by the Serpents.

When souls are incorporated into the bodies that are in storage, the soul can be allowed to sleep. Some souls are kept entertained with visions of past lives; good if the lives were pleasant, very bad if lives were repulsive and painful. Programing concerning their new lives on Earth is installed weeks prior to being released onto the planet.

The new programming overlaps, removes, or erases past memories, allowing for a transition period in the new environment. Most times the new inhabitants were unaware they were placed on a different planet (they had no way of knowing, even without the cerebral programming that wiped away previous memories).

Humans or humanized Martians, were provide with leadership skills and allowed to take over weaker human and subhuman tribes and societies that they came upon. Serpents made frequent deposits on Earth of such barbaric tribes, spanning periods of thousands of years before the last major Ice Age. Many additional deposits came after the last major Ice Age (and the accompanying worldwide floods, created by receding glaciers).

The destruction of homogenized Martian societies by the Serpents left Martians on the brink of extinction. Deprived of technology by the Serpents, many of the surviving Martian clans lapsed intellectually and technologically and became as beasts. Numerous Martian clans were deposited on Earth by the Serpents (as a seed reserve for genetic material, and a number of other unmentionable reasons).

Martians roamed the Earth as hunters, killing animals and other lesser humanoids for food. Martian tribes tamed wild roaming animals for domestic use, turning them into beasts of burden, as well as a maintainable and readily available food source. During the course of time, Martians underwent mutations that were provoked by the Serpents, to facilitate primate/human lineages.

Serpents were granted access to higher knowledge and given increased technological abilities to manage the Neanderthals (Martians). And to homogenize Homo sapiens, from the stock of refugees, from planet Man, and mating them with various races from galactic hot-spots in other parts of the galaxy.

Some primate species and numerous other animal types were salvaged from planet Man before it was destroyed, and they were reestablished on Earth and Mars, along with the human equivalents (prototypes).

Martian ruins covered the Martian surface for eons after Mars was attacked by the Serpents, and left desolated. Remnants of cities and the bones of Martians and other creatures that were not incinerated by the Serpents, slowly dissolved in the abrasive Martian winds. Remnants remain and are strewn across some of the Martian landscape. Most vestiges are buried deep in the Martian soil or lie loose in the many caverns and caves inside Mar's vast interior.

The once powerful civilization on Mars was reduced to fragmented ghettoes of Martian clans. Martian refugees rummaged amongst the rubble and the dust of structures and cities for food that had become scarce, and for the shelter that provided little security. Many of the surviving Martians were moved to caverns beneath the Martian surface by their new masters, the Serpents. Martians were allowed to subsist and exist in miserable conditions until they were relocated to other planets and moons in the star system, where they were used as breeding stock and combatants; for the general purpose of eradicating and assimilating other species of beings within their tribes and clans.

Martians were enslaved and used as labor, warriors and for hybridization with native beings on the planets and moons they were relocated to.

Numerous Martians managed to escape the Serpent onslaught (before and after) and hid deep inside the interior of Mars, where they sometimes found refuge in the extensive labyrinth of mines and caves.

Martians who were away from the planet and away from the Martian colonies, when the Serpents attacked, retained some autonomy, along with their mental faculties and skills. Those Martians had technological abilities and advanced ships that they continued to use for survival during deep space excursions. A few Martians found refuge at the outer edges of the star system inside large chunks of rocks, the remnants of destroyed planets and moons that make up a massive halo encircling the star system.

Hundreds of thousands of intact planetoids and moons on the outskirts of the star system are populated with bizarre creatures that are mysterious and fierce and avoided by the normally fearless Martians. Martians also hid among, and found refuge in the remains of planet Man, and the moons that now make up the asteroid belt.

Martian survivors (allowed by the Serpents to survive) reside on most of the inner planets and moons in the star system. Martians were occasionally discovered alongside Renegade encampments, where they receive shelter, aid, training and sometimes betrayal, death, and slaughter, by their unpredictable hosts, in the halo zone that surrounds the star system.

Martians foraged in the scrub of ancient forests that once covered Mars, and scavenged materials from the ruined Martian cities to build surface and underground habitats.

Select breeds of young Martians (those previously infused with compatible genes to humans) were culled from villages and taken to Earth and other planets in the star system; by the Serpents, to populate and intermix with humans. Periodic, and sequentially, throughout the centuries on Earth, Martians were dropped off, and turned loose, to ravage and vanquish plague-ridden races in the regions they were given as an inheritance.

Martians subsequently introduced the smelting of iron to humans through the conquering of human cities and societies and adapting to human cultures and ways.

The Iron Age was only a reintroduction of iron to the planet Earth. Bronze, iron, and other metals are innate to earth and native to all planets and moons in the star system. Iron was prized and used by waves of Renegades that have come and gone in the millions of years before the implementation of modern humans on Earth. The ability and knowledge to turn base metals into fighting implements, and for use in agriculture and industry was calculated and timed by the overlords, who steadily disseminated bits of knowledge to earthlings.

Mars had one large moon that was destroyed during the attack by the Serpents. Some of the moon fragments fell to Mars and the rest scattered to other inner and outer planets and moons, in the form of meteors and solar dust.

Earth received sporadic shipments of Martian hybrids, post-Neanderthal stage, and again in several stages after the world-wide floods. Flood waters from the melting ice wiped away (killed off) several tail-end, late civilizations of humanoids that were placed on Earth ages earlier. Martians and humans that had intermixed with Renegades and spawned mixtures of human and animal hybrids, for barbaric games and spare parts (for those damaged in the games). Human/animal hybrids were used in battles and to track down creatures brought to earth by Renegades.

Perverse sexual diversions created by, and for Renegade hybrids, was an exploited venture for most of the existing races on some level. It was a remnant pestilence that existed before the floodwaters that wiped away many of the early encampments and villages, of the gore-driven beings, and their genetically engineered monstrous creatures.

Martians adapted to colder climates after the near destruction of their race and the planet. A major setback that left Martians unequipped to deal with the reduction of solar heat (the sun transitioned and entered a calmer and cooler stage, which brought on the recent Ice Age on Earth. Martians that were resettled on Earth were deposited in northern climates; climates that were suitable for them after their decline on Mars, eons earlier.

Batches of Martians shipped to Earth were specifically bred to coincide with the race of humans they were meant to encounter, conquer, and mate with. Martians were aggressive by nature and became more so because of the despairing conditions they were placed into by the Serpents. Martians pillaged, subjugated, and displaced most of the races (human or otherwise), that they made contact with. Martians killed the males and impregnated the females, spawning new breeds of humans that were later hunted and destroyed by the Serpents, or the countless numbers of mercenaries that were employed by the Serpents.

BIGFOOT

Martians that were sent to other planets and moons in the star system were tailored to coincide with the destination and the natives. Martians were used on projects that differed from what they did on Earth. Some Martians tended to be solitary and preferred to work alone when given the choice. Their demeanor and physiology favored them being placed into harsh and cold places on distant planets and moons, working as scouts and combatants for the Serpents. Some Martians understood their missions; most didn't know that they were working for the Serpents, through surrogate (middlemen) beings. And inadvertently some Martians collected information on other Martians, along with the beings they infiltrated (for the clandestine beings secretly aligned with Serpents).

Martians are exceptional survivalists and able to subsist on assorted and meager diets for long periods, and under most weather conditions (preferably cold). A branch of modern Martians are known as Yetis, Bigfoot, Sasquatch, and Abominable, by unsuspecting modern humans, who believed such beasts to be myths, and if not myths, then exotic and extremely illusive creatures of Earth.

Martian creatures of the Bigfoot variety, are frequently spotted in isolated places on earth, by hunters and campers, who mistakenly believe that they have stumbled on the strange and reclusive creatures by accident.

Accidental encounters with the creatures are rare if they exist at all. Sasquatch type creatures have prequalified the mortal humans, and set up the encounter with specific humans in mind, for the sole purpose and usage of Sasquatch. Yetis make use of the humans they search out, summoning them to areas where they will then extract human byproducts, and other materials from humans or animals that they need while on Earth, and for the return trip back from where they came.

Yetis are more technologically advanced than their genetically equivalent humans. Secretions from various human organs are extracted by Yetis, who use the bile and other biological material "borrowed" from their close cousins, humans (that are adapted to Earth conditions). Yeti supplements specific organic requirements homogenized to earthly conditions by the human body (to metabolize food ingestion) during their brief expeditions on Earth (human yogurt, yum).

Human fluids allow a Yeti to acclimate rapidly to the regional environment it is placed into or that it enters into on its own accord.

Planets and moons have unique gravitational qualities, pressures, and climates, which impair and challenge humanoid bodies that are not internally equipped for "all" the rapid changes and conditions they will encounter. Spacesuits help for those with advanced space suits, but not all Yeti creatures use spacesuits. Bigfoot creatures that do use spacesuits use suits that are crafted to look like a large hairy beast, which sometimes hides a large hairy beast inside of them but not always. Sasquatches easily acclimate to whatever environment they find themselves in by tapping into the local pool of inhabitants that share similar biological functions; on Earth that would be humans and other primates. Most of the time, humans and animals are not killed or damaged by the Martian creatures, only tapped for biological ingredients, and then turned loose.

Abominable beings come and go from planets and moons using highly advanced spaceships (UFOs). And have similar abduction capabilities (over humans) as do other higher or lower extraterrestrials beings, who are trafficking goods and services in the local star system, and beyond.

Bigfoots have taken humans and animals off the planet for various and unknown reasons, and then returned the humans unharmed (most of the time) back to their place of origin. Nefarious Bigfoots have taken people and not returned them (at the direction of black ops coverts), from Earth, and transplanted the humans on other planets and moons for use by higher and lower echelon entities. It is but one of many types of slave trading operations in this star system that is run independently and illegally by multiple renegade tribes. Sometimes sanctioned or done under contract at the discretion of the gods or the Serpents.

Entering and leaving planets and moons is risky for most types of beings. Regardless of the level of technological sophistication, they might possess, and casualties happened more often than not. Hostilities between higher and lower beings is a constant danger to most itinerant beings, and their hostages or companions. On numerous occasions, humans have been victims in the mayhem of engagement, and exchange of fire, while in the possession of the beings that have abducted them. Such fatalities result in the disappearance of thousands of humans (and other beings, creatures, and animals) each year from the planet Earth, and other planets and moons in the star system.

Martians are one of many foreign species allowed to mingle with the human race and become part of the human race. Renegade Alien beings were permitted to slip through Earth's defenses and claim Earth as a temporary hovel during ancient times and present times as well.

Serpents used the intruders (who were sometimes clueless that they were being used) and wove them into the fabric of humanity; as part of the architecture of a future multiracial planet (the one that exists now), and for future times, when humans will break free from earth and enter space in ever larger numbers.

Future space exploring humans will face encounters that will stretch their minds and souls to breathtaking heights and delights. And to breaking points of fear and despair of the crazy beings and creature-things that are out there, loose and lurking everywhere in space. Humans will learn that childhood myths, fables, and legends, of the strange, bizarre, and creepy, are words without meaning. In other words, myths, fables, and legends are real, and not mythical at all.

Renegades were brought to the star system by messengers of the overseers and placed onto various planets and moons. Renegades, the displaced beings from star systems within the Milky Way, are exiled beings from their home planets, due to crimes and infractions against their own people. Renegades come from technologically advanced planets and cultures and retained portions of their former superior technological abilities.

Renegade societies on Earth have flourished (covertly) because of their high-tech advantages over human and Martian population. Renegades enslaved humans and Martians, bred with them, and farmed them out to other renegades, to increase inhabitants for labor, food cultivation, the slave trade, and to raise armies, as well as for genetic properties.

Renegades use(d) flying machines (aircraft) and other more advanced ships (UFOs) that allowed them access to other planets, moons and space cities, to conduct their affairs within this star system (privileges often allowed them by the gods).

Renegades inject mischief and war wherever they invade and accumulate. Occasionally, Renegades are disciplined or destroyed by Serpents, and other Reptilian beings, that are garrisoned throughout this star system, for security reasons. Some Renegades are of the Reptilian and Serpent breeds. Breeds of entities that have succumbed to corruption and were exiled by their own races; and later captured and quarantined to this star system and placed in servitude to Serpents; who sometimes sublet them to dark forces and other low-end creepy creatures.

PLANET MAN

Planet Man had a population of over100 billion humans at the time of its demise. Several billion additional humans from Man lived on the four moons, and the numerous space cities and outposts on moons and planets, which were dispersed throughout the star system. Humans that were located off-planet were randomly hunted, killed and captured by Martians during the extended period of wars before the destruction of planet Man, and its moons.

Planet man was densely populated, meaning that the interior of the planet was like Swiss cheese, and lined with layers of cities built inside of large caverns that made up the inside of planet Man. Sunlight streamed to the interior of the planet from large surface openings that channeled sunlight to every niche and cranny inside of the planet. Sunlight flooded the interior cities with sun and warmth making the cities seem as if they were above ground.

Numerous, large, atrium shafts, whose length reached down to the center of planet Man, thousands of feet into the interior, with the other end protruding thousands of feet above the surface, to the very edge of space, dominated planet Man's land and oceans.

Additionally to the shafts reaching into space, huge slabs of glass, covering low-lying structures, enclosed parts of the planet and parts of the oceans. Other structures that supplemented the surface openings, to let in the sun, were humongous open air holes, which were carved into the ground. The holes enabled air intake to the lowest inner regions of Man, as well as allowing the sunshine to reach the vast internal network of tunnels and spaces inside the abyss of the planet.

Within the atriums and surface openings, massive elevators moved large numbers of people and materials swiftly from surface to interior and exterior, and into space. Elevators operated both horizontally and vertically, and connected all the cities to the atriums and surface openings. At the top of the atriums were space platforms that connected to a web of cities and an extensive array of incredibly busy spaceports.

Humans were comprehensively involved in every aspect and activity that was taking place throughout the star system. Humans enjoyed unparalleled prosperity and interacted with nearly all physical beings that were conducting interstellar and domestic commerce. Humans had knowledge about and controlled enormous quantities of resources on planet man, Man's four moons, and the numerous planets and moons beyond planet Pluto (in addition to all the inner planets and moons).

Humans acted as facilitators and the ones to go to, to get things done in the overt world. They were the middlemen of the star system, exchanging currencies and facilitating deals between various internal races and classes of beings; transacting with beings and races in far-off star systems. Humans had a prime and exclusive position in the star system that kept dealings between beings above board. Humans created a sense of safety and integrity in a star system that was wilder and more lawless than any Wild West scenario.

Not all humans were equipped with spacefaring bodies and capabilities. But all humans could spend limited time at the top of atriums and visit, or vacation in the space cities that were connected to the spaceports docked to planet Man.

Humans that were categorized to live in distant space cities and other harsh environments that were dissimilar to conditions on planet Man received modified bodies at birth. The bodies were designed to withstand space atmospheres as well as conditions on planet Man. Nevertheless, the majority of spacefaring humans, while at their home planet, and between assignments, chose to live in one of the thousands of space cities orbiting planet Man, rather than live on the surface of the planet.

The civilization of Man was not utopic (utopia) but close to it. Humans on Man had space-age technology that was supplied to them from higher beings residing at the periphery of the star system (the gods or their sidekicks, the Serpents).

Humans of Man were fair skinned and with above average physique. Humans lacked in the hair department. But had a little hair around the groin region, and no hair on most of the body, except for the head. Some humans chose to have hair on their heads. However, most were bald (male and female).

Nudity was common, and the dress was limited to robes and other loose clothing when it was worn. There was no need or desire for restrictive undergarments. Human bodies didn't sag, become obese or produce odors. Nevertheless, bathing was popular, convenient and fun, for all humans. Bathhouses were plentiful and located throughout the city, where people congregated, in parks, commercial buildings, and in residential units (on or off planet).

Humans were made in the image of the gods, and had bodies that metabolized most of the food and beverage they consumed. Humans of Man did not create bodily waste to the extent that Earth humans do. Males stood approximately six feet tall, slender and handsome; females were a few inches shorter, typically slim, and attractive. The battle between the sexes didn't exist. Everyone was happy with who they were, without having to compete with each other. Variations in height and body shape could be found and depended on where the humans resided most of the time during their lives. Living in different environments, moons, space cities and deep in the interior of the planet, affected human physiology, and to a degree, psychologically.

Man's history was linear with no evolution or theories of how things came into existence. Humans knew what they needed to know about their place in the star system and no more. Everything was as it seemed (or so it was believed by the whole population). Topics as religion, evolution and philosophy, were not in the vocabulary of Man's humans.

Humans were born and taken care of by the parents that gave them birth, until adulthood (reached a few years after puberty). After which time the progeny went out on their own, and repeated the process of creating families with chosen mates (chosen by parents). Couples copulated for life but were free to mingle with other humans, sexually and socially. Only couples genetically mated to each other could produce offspring.

Sexuality was for procreation and for pleasure. Sex was engaged in by all, with no misconceptions, taboos or restrictions. Only mature humans wishing to have children gave birth to children (most of the population bore children). Abortions or destruction of embryos was unnecessary and never happened.

Humans didn't worship gods or engage in rituals of any kind. There was no need for political debate, political parties or leaders; everyone understood the rules and everyone abided by the rules. No crime, and therefore no prisons existed on planet Man, or on any of its moons, subsidiaries, jurisdictions, or colonies (until the wars broke out between Humans and Martians, in which case, it was handled by the Serpents).

Open hostilities towards humans by Martians ended when the Serpents obliterated planet Man and most of Man's human populations centers scattered around the star system. Martian aggressions directed at humans on some of Man's colonies were dealt with by the Serpents, who protected humans up until they were ordered to destroy the humans.

Planet Man had healthcare, and hospitals and all humans regularly frequented nearby clinics as part of their normal routines. Accidents happened and a few diseases and other ailments afflicted some humans, primarily in the colonies deep in space. (Trivial disorders compared to human ailments on modern Earth).

Human visits to medical facilities were part of the upbringing and conditioning of humans. Visits with medical staff had little to do with health issues and more to do with monitoring the human contact with other beings, more so, reptilian beings.

Humans were unaware of the true nature of the medical visits that they underwent their entire lives. Doctors removed specific Reptilian parasites and left other alien organisms intact inside the humans. The parasites that were removed had peculiar monitoring applications that were not allowed by the Serpents.

Humans lived relatively long, healthy, lives and were mentally and physically fit for more than a century of their existence. Death was not traumatic since most humans lived to the ripe old age of a century and a half. Fatalities and early death were unheard of or rare (other than deliberate attacks by Martians and other beings). Humans on Man were unaware of the soul and the afterlife and believed that death was final (A belief that is common with many modern humans).

Public transportation connected cities and towns around the planet and was the primary means of people getting from one place to another. Self-driving robotic vehicles existed mostly for transport of materials and goods, and not for personal use. Personal vehicles were not allowed inside population centers but were prevalent in designated and undeveloped areas that were set aside for off-road type vehicles, for recreational activities.

Planet Man rotated on its axis with much of the landmass over the equator. Oceans and icecaps encircled the poles and were the epitome of winter wonderlands. The weather was tropical and pleasant throughout the year for much of the planet. Weather and storms, such as tornadoes, hurricanes, and earthquakes, were managed and controlled by the Serpents, and rarely destructive or severe.

Population centers were concentrated on the landmass and on the thousands of floating cities on the ocean. In the oceans (massive submarine-cities constantly moved around the oceans), and domed cities were built into the ocean floors. Cities submerged below the oceans, those stationary and the submarines, made up a substantial part of the human habitat.

Water was a desirable attraction to humans, primarily because of the extraordinary views of aquatic creatures and the endless variety of exotic sea life that enveloped submerged structures. Swarms of glowing and monstrous-sized squid and myriads of different types and species of electrified and colorful jellyfish made for one of the many nonstop visual activities humans took pleasure in. Varieties of fish and other types of aquatic life numbered in the millions, and new species were created and added periodically, while some species were eliminated for various reasons.

Aquatic activities, such as swimming, snorkeling, scuba diving and boating, were routine and enjoyed by most humans. Water was never far away, and was always conveniently located. Whether it was natural or manmade, lakes and other bodies of water existed wherever humans resided.

Underground cities and the colonies in space provided considerable and endless real estate for planet Man's population to expand into. People of Man continued their substantial expansion into space over the hundreds of thousands of years that humans existed on Man.

Elusive prodding from Reptilians was behind many choices that determined where humans ended up creating colonies. Reptilians were and are everywhere in the star system, and remain mostly incognito, out of sight and out of mind, of the humans, in the past and the present-day too. Some Martian hybrids were able to detect the presence of Reptilians but were unable to stop them from doing whatever they intended to do with them.

Dinosaurs and other exotic animals and creatures existed in isolated areas on Man. The behemoths were viewed from flying ships and from platforms by the humans, for entertainment and recreation.

Earth was not always open and available to humans from Man, which cut off access to the planetary zoo that was Earth, for eons. After the wars began and made space travel hazardous for all beings, humans avoided going to Earth, where much of the hostilities and fighting was ongoing.

Humans from Man, in comparison to Martians, Serpents, and Reptilians, were bred to be pacifists. Man's military was defensive and consisted of androids and drones provided and maintained by the Serpents (foxes guarding the chicken coop).

Food production on Man was comprised of animal protein and vegetation, same as on Earth. Numerous animal species, including fish and fowl, were farmed industrially by machines and kept out of sight and mind of humans. Humans enjoyed the end product at grocery stores and restaurants, similarly to today's' humans. Artificial food production (replicators) were supplemental, and part of the appliances in kitchens and public transportation systems, where human food was served.

Synthetic foods were abundant and mostly for use by the humans in space. Still, many humans preferred the real meat and potatoes, over artificial food. Humans were free to eat whatever they wanted to eat, and diverse diets existed among the population.

Planet Man catered to human populations for millions of years, with little change or upgrade in technology, and topography. Chronologically, Man was static, prehistory and future time concepts didn't exist. However, populations were purged, replaced and rotated every few hundred thousand years, or so, to clean out mutations and gene manipulations done by various parasitic creatures and beings that sporadically leached onto humans.

Upon death, humans were cremated, and their ashes returned to the ground. Burials, memorials, and headstones had no meaning and were not used. Life on Man was standardized and saw little changed in economic conditions or any conditions. Humans didn't experience poverty or ignorance and were sheltered from such concepts and realities.

A self-perpetuating economic system was in place on Man, placed there and sustained by higher beings (Serpents) working for the overseers (gods).

Gods could be found everywhere in the star system, enjoying their lives while riding inside of palatial starships, and cruising the star system or living in palatial cities that were located on every planet and moon in the system, and created for their exclusive use.

Reptilians were reliant on Man's humans for biological secretions and genetic cocktails. Reptilians had a symbiotic relationship with humans that benefited both the humans and the Reptilians. Humans were unaware of that relationship or any contact with Reptilians other than during a business transaction. Humans did not know them as Reptilians since Reptilians are masters of mascaraed (then and now). Humans were aware of certain reptilian beings, the Serpents, who were profoundly involved in all human affairs, and other types of hybridized reptilian beings, that they only dealt with occasionally, in the matters of administration and exchange of materials, goods, and services.

Reptilians carried out their deeds subtly without human awareness or interference (by the Serpents). Humans were easily subdued (abducted) during the night when they were sleeping. Transactions were short lived, and the humans returned to their sleeping quarters never realizing a transaction (abduction) took place. Reptilians removed specific enzymes, and in turn placed beneficial hormones into the abducted humans. The hormones helped keep the humans healthy, calm, euphoric and unaware of their sojourns with Reptilians. It was a mutually advantageous transaction, sort of akin to the care given to dairy cows so that the milk supply remained consistent and plentiful (for the Reptilians). The tradeoff left humans emotionally sound and content for the entirety of their lives.

Human bodies from Man were designed to produce various enzymes, as well as large amounts of eggs and semen. Reptilians exploited the rich human biological resource that was readily available in every corner of the star system, due in part to Reptilian influences.

Unlike modern versions of humans, the bodies of human females of Man produced thousands of eggs in their oversized ovaries and expelled the unused eggs more frequently than earth-human female-equivalents, do. Males produced copious amounts of sperm, far more than modern human males, and it had to be expelled more frequently. Intercourse was routine and everyone keen on sexual interaction whenever and wherever. The result was that the human population continually expanded and was readily available anywhere in the star system (by the design of the gods). Humans were not a food source, but they were containers of more than souls. Humans were rich in biological material and repositories essential for the Reptilians, and also for the gods.

Males of Man copulated primarily with one or two females (the core of the typical Man family). But males were free to copulate with other females, and females were free to indulge other males and females, for pleasure only. The primary couple was the only ones that could give birth to offspring. Dalliances with other males or females could not result in pregnancy. Primary couples were genetically matched to reproduce children and could not produce children with others. It was a genetic arrangement that made it impossible for defects to happen in offspring. Children were hereditarily near perfect under the birthing system on Man, and all of Mans' colonies. Child producing couples could stop producing children whenever they wished by engaging with others not mated to them. Couples wishing to maintain sexual intimacy without creating children with their matched partners took a pill or had a simple and reversible procedure performed at the clinic.

Marriage and ceremonies to bind humans to each other weren't practiced on Man. Love, desire and genetically harmonized, is what fused humans on Man (till death did them in). Young couples began a life together at various ages after puberty. They received modest accommodation when they first started out, and the accommodations expanded as families grew in size.

Typical families numbered more than five children and increased for some couples to more than twenty children, all living under the same roof. As families increased they moved to larger apartments or houses, whichever they preferred. Most families lived in large metropolitan cities with populations in the millions. There were smaller urban and suburban communities, as well as country and forest living, for those that preferred nature and seclusion.

Human bodies were designed for pleasure and giving birth was a pleasurable experience. Sexual deviance was nonexistent. Sex was a normal part of human life, and all humans were free to explore sexual activity. Negative emotions concerning sexuality were not programmed into the human mind by the higher beings, who created the emotion software for the humans on Man, as well as the emotion software for modern human populations on Earth.

All humans born under Man's jurisdiction (throughout the star system) were provided for from the moment of birth until death, by an apparatus created and put into place by the gods. Work, schooling and chosen/preferred professions, hobby or otherwise, were a choice. Humans could spend their whole lives in leisure type activities, which most humans did.

Crime and punishment were unheard of. Everyone had what they needed and wanted, which eliminated resentment and discord. Sex was natural and accessible to all, negating sex crimes between humans. Economic situations were near perfect and domestic violence, and violence of any kind between humans was absent.

Human bodies (containers) hosted microbes important to the gods; and the organic life that was prevalent in the star system. The gods created vast quantities of microbes and stored them inside of living creatures (human bodies and the bodies of the pets the humans owned). Preserving and making available a biological trove (by propagating humans and other creatures in the star system) was part of a cosmic ecosystem that benefited other beings and creatures that were not of the humanoid variety.

Reptilians were part of the cosmic ecosystem, and acted as pollinators and accelerants of microbes when they came into contact with humans, and other beings and creatures, during their space travels. Acting as pollen-laden bees, contaminated Reptilians spread the microbes to other star systems, pollinating as they made their journeys through the stars, like insects going from one flowering plant to the next.

Microbes with recombinant DNA, are kept alive and well inside the Reptilian bodies, and later the carcasses, that are left to drift in the deep spaces of space, where star systems marinate in the juices of various microbes. Reptilians live long healthy lives lasting hundreds of years. When Reptilians approach the end of their lives and are about to die (they know the time of their "natural" death), they set themselves (their bodies) adrift between the stars.

Existing within Reptilian carcasses, microbes remain alive forever and are eventually swept up by new and existing planetary systems, within star systems, and the planetary systems outside of the gravitational clutches of stars. Such microbes provide the primary basis for ecological growth to new and barren planets. After many millennia, gods move in and set up shop, adding plant and animal life (the forerunners of things to come).

The vast majority of planets and moons in the universe reside in the vast regions of space between star systems. Discarded planets that were born from various types of stars and have escaped the star's gravitational field. And planets that were jettisoned from the stars spit out with such velocities during sun flairs and overshoot the edge of star systems. Such vagabond planets, moons and other solar ejecta, whose remnants and debris from collisions with other space rubble, are the stuffing between the stars. Eventually, over millions of years, much of the loose matter gets absorbed back into star systems, in the form of comets and asteroids, from which planets and moons gorge on.

Star birth (formation) happens at the core of galaxies, where stars are spewed from black holes or white holes, as frequently and as pervasively as spawning fish.

Space cities had the same human amenities and comforts that were on planet Man. Schools, luxurious apartments, medical facilities, and abundant flora and fauna (plants and animals). Fantastic zoos and enchanted parks added and expanded a sense of peace and tranquility to the humans adrift in faraway places.

Pets were part of the human existence and accompanied humans on their distant travels. Varieties of aquatic life and non-aquatic pets, similar to cats, dogs and numerous other types of biological and synthetic creatures, were abundant and played a significant part in the human scheme. Biological pets were engineered to be low maintenance or no maintenance and provided additional comforts to humans, and the overall ecological system that is existing inside of spaceships and space cities.

Each city, planetary or in deep space, had its own food production facilities that provided fresh vegetables, fruits, meat, poultry, fish and numerous other exotic delights (not available to modern humans on Earth).

Food production, labor, and manufacturing of all kinds, was mechanized, leaving humans with time to do what they enjoyed doing, without mundane labor or worries. Leisure, learning, games, reproduction, and indulging in sexual activities were daily doings of the masses.

Some humans chose to do jobs in the fields of engineering, teaching, and other scientific arenas. But classifying human activities and endeavors "work" is a stretch. Most of the real work was carried out by androids and other types of highly advanced biological, synthetic and mechanical contraptions. Gods and Serpents handled much of the managerial and technical requirements of running the human race, but humans were free to engage in activities of their choosing.

The legislative procedure, courts of law, lawyers and legal complexities, which muddle the modern human masses on Earth, didn't exist on planet Man.

Means of production and the ownership of designs belonged to the technological wizards (the gods) who provided everything needed, wanted or desired, to the entirety of the humans race.

Humans were pampered for the same reasons that well fed, healthy bodies, and gratified souls (together), provided needed superior biological materials to a wide and varied range of interested parties, not least, to higher echelon beings, existing beyond the stars, which never even visited star systems.

Basic knowledge was achieved from devices implanted into children at birth by the parents. Learning was augmented by playing with complex interactive toys, and taking several mind-expanding adventure trips to cosmic retreats. Adults never stopped learning, which was a pleasurable activity. Learning happened while doing whatever the adult wished to do: play musical instruments, paint, sculpt, mountain climb, swim, fish, or any number of pleasurable undertakings.

Accomplishments and showcasing talents held little meaning other than individual amusement. Egoism and self-importance were emotions lacking in humans of Man.

Humans existed to enjoy the pleasures of physical life for a set number of years, roughly about 150 earth years. The long life allowed humans to engage with several generations of family members during one lifetime. Long life also contributed to the real purpose of humans, which was procreate and expand the human race to the far corners of the star system.

Humans weren't challenged or tested for endurance, proficiency, morality, intelligence, spirituality, or virtue. All those things were innate, built into the human mind and body by the gods. Hate, envy, greed, lust, depravity, corruption, evil and all other vices or malicious intents, did not afflict human souls of that particular breed, during the epoch of Man.

Humans existed in a bubble, protected from hostile beings (for the most part) that lusted after what humans had, and came easily to them.

Humans had it all, health and happiness, enormous resources, and riches beyond belief. Cities of gold and overflowing with copious amounts of diamonds and other precious stones and jewels. The hoard of metals, natural and synthetics adorned individuals, their habitats and the cities they lived in.

Humans had an affinity for things of beauty. Sculptures, paintings, architecture and jewelry, mostly created by other beings on other planets, were prized and sought after by humans. Humans were no less materialistic than most highly advanced beings, which traded and traveled between the stars.

Planet Man was covered in unspoiled forests of old growth trees, some dating back thousands of years. Most trees were not harvested, but there was high demand for exotic woods, from humans and tourists. There was no shortage of exotic woods, and large quantities of lumber were imported from some of Man's moons to the many human colonies in the system.

Rainforests, mountains, waterfalls, rivers and streams were part of the simple pleasures humans enjoyed. Tame wildlife and colorful insects added a magical atmosphere to the forest experience. Biting insects were designed without the bite (for humans) and dangerous animals only existed within zoo habitats. Public forests were havens for numerous types of animals that were free to roam and hunt in a perfectly balanced ecosystem.

Renewable exotic woods were harvested, used and valued in jewelry, furniture and interiors of homes, and public buildings. Enchanted, synthetic materials that glowed with multiple colors, and radiated sounds and music of one's desires, was incorporated into the structures, homes, and buildings that humans occupied.

Wood was burned in fireplaces and on camping trips for the same sentimental reasons modern humans cherish the warm glow and crackle of burning wood. Fake fireplaces or any number of scenes or scenery could be projected on any wall in every room of a human abode, but a real fire never lost its appeal.

Palatial buildings and homes were made with metallic alloys, stone, marble, ceramics, wood, glass, plastics, and various colorful types of concrete materials. Towns and villages were decorated with many types of architectural designs and were peppered between the landscapes of massive superstructures that shot straight up several miles into the stratosphere. The superstructures had large footprints that covered several acres of land. Thousands of such structures held the housing and activities areas for millions of humans. Most of the structures were uniform, and detached from each other, and were connected by enclosed walkways and underground links. Superstructures were coupled to the underground cities and connected directly to spaceports and space cities above the planet.

Human colonies dispersed in the planetary system consisted of groups of families that joined together and embarked on voyages that lasted several generations. Colonies on planets and moons experienced several cycles of families, friends and associates, who remained stationary (stayed put). More adventurous families traveled to other planets and moons and through the vast space that separates planets and moons. Some families traveled throughout the star system with only immediate family, in ships much larger and more technologically advanced than what the fictional "Lost in Space", Robinson family, had.

A typical family-classed ship had several levels on it, and each level was the size of two or three gymnasiums. Huge, and plenty of space for a growing family. When members of the family reached a certain age, they often moved out and started their own family. Therefore, families hardly ever outgrew their ships. If they did, they could upgrade to a larger ship.

Ship interiors were mostly open spaces, with eating areas, family rooms, and activity rooms, on the main level. Sleeping quarters and workspaces were located on other levels.

The temperature inside the ship stayed the same and was near that of the humans, which was a degree or two lower than modern humans. Those on the ship wore nothing or only a silk robe if they did. Bathrooms had no meaning, and toilets were in the open and available in several locations on each level. Toilets were simple pods that looked like upturned mushrooms, with a cup-of-a-hand stool, that was sat on.

When humans had to go, they sat on the rubbery cup and it conformed and closed around the buttocks and private parts (nothing was private). Bidets, toilet paper or sinks to wash hands, were absent and unnecessary. Little tikes had a similar device that wrapped around their bottoms, and kept them dry and clean, without ever needing a change. Humans walking in space or leaving the ship wore spacesuits or plain suits, equipped with biodegradable catch-all underwear, which like the magical high-tech diapers, didn't need changing or emptying. Poop and urine biodegraded away, inside the wearable microbiological devices.

Pools, a type of large hot tub, was located on each level and inside every bedroom. Pools were for cleansing and relaxing in. Humans were genetically designed to be stress-free and were always relaxed. So bathing in water served other benign purposes. Humans socialized while soaking in warm saltwater pools.

Ships didn't have control panels, cockpits or control centers. Pertinent information, news, and entertainment displayed itself on windows, walls, floors, and ceilings and on roaming drones. Information was also communicated to humans through self-implanted microscopic and biological communications devices. Technically, all information was transmitted telepathically. Humans were in constant contact with each other (on some level), no matter the distance from their home planet of Man, or anywhere in the star system.

Humans enjoyed various sounds and music inside the ships and wherever humans were, waves of sound and spectrums of light enveloped them. Ships had more mojo because they moved through space at fantastic speeds, creating mind-numbing colorful displays of unimaginable light shows that clung and danced on the translucent skin of the ship. The electrifying sound and graceful light of the magic-show was visible to the occupants no matter where they were on the ship.

Customized spaceships were provided to the humans on Man, and were in the magical category concerning technological capabilities. Serpents supplied the technology for the ships and the androids to construct and maintain the ships. Humans didn't input much or anything other than command the ship where to take them. Ships were nearly indestructible, and accidents extremely rare. However, Serpents, gods, and other high-level beings have the power to destroy whatever they deem needs destroying.

DESTRUCTION OF PLANET MAN

The destruction of planet Man, a planet twice the size of Earth, and two of its four moons was catastrophic to the extreme. The explosion that incinerated the planet, two of its moons, and the billions of humans on them, unleashed horror into the hearts and minds of all sentient beings, who were aware of the devastation. It was a near instantaneous eradication of nearly all humans in the star system. Humans didn't see it coming, sparing them the anguish.

Chunks and fragments from the moons and the planet created storms of meteor showers on the remaining inner and outer planets and their moons. Intense meteor showers persisted for hundreds of thousands of years after the explosion of Man and continued to this day (with far less intensity). And the bombardment of material will persist for eons into the future. Much of the material has already fallen (a long time ago) onto the inner planets, Mars, Earth, Venus, Mercury, Earth's moon, and the sun, and have been absorbed and become part of those celestial bodies.

The four moons and the planet, Man, were populated primarily by human type beings but hundreds of thousands of other kinds of beings on Man, and on the moons, perished with the humans. Planet Man and the two moons were annihilated by the Serpents, on orders from higher authorities in the galaxy.

Serpents exterminated much of the life on planet Man moments before blowing it up. Humans had become genetically obtuse over the millions of years of subtle manipulation by obscure Reptilian beings, and the excessive pampering by the gods. The planet and four moons received lethal doses of bacteria that caused the human populations to die rapidly and decompose. The two surviving moons, and some of the larger chunks of the planet, and moons continue to have non-human elements on them. Elements that acted as cleansing agents to eradicate vestiges of humans and other beings.

The dispersed humans throughout the star system were eradicated by the Serpents, at the same instant as those on Man and its moons. Serpents employed large numbers of renegade militias that were already in place (garrisoned throughout the star system). They swiftly assassinated the humans and destroyed their millions of colonies and spaceships in the whole of the system.

Planet Man's utopic ways conflicted with the new protocol in the star system. The declaration dictated a stage of the demise of the old ways to make room for a birth of sequential breeds of humanoids to be placed on planet Earth. It was part of a revamping period that was underway before the obliteration of Humans. The decree profoundly affected the whole star system and the multitudes of life forms still residing in it.

Before the attack on Man, and the elimination of the
human population, Serpents moved and placed into quarantine
large numbers of humans. Humans were placed in enormous
container ships, to preserve the human bodies for future genetic
use. The souls were removed and the human bodies placed into
a state of suspension, where bodies remained alive in a
cryogenic-type state, indefinitely.

After the destruction of the human race, the revised
human model (pre-modern human) received a different type of
soul, one that was used on Earth thousands of years before
modern humans existed. Souls of yet another branch were
activated for modern humans.

The billions of souls released at the moment of the
human annihilation produced a shockwave of psychic energy
that flowed from this star system and moved as an immense
high-frequency cloud to a place near the center of the galaxy.
Where the souls joined with families of humans that had passed
away over the eons of Man's existence. From there, and after a
time, souls were assigned to other physical lives throughout the
galaxy. Some souls came back to this star system and incarnated
on Earth. Souls from Man continued to arrive on Earth over the

span of several centuries and into the present age of modern humans.

Human souls had it easy while on Man and during the entire epoch of Man, and were not tested or tormented. That changed after the fall of Man.

When the time came, clans of the reengineered, and soulless human bodies (that were in storage) were reawakened and dropped off on Earth and allowed to roam and forage under Serpent supervision. Human bodies were provided a different soul and received a degree of protections from the Renegades that roamed freely on the face of the Earth, during that transformation period.

From the stock of humans in cryogenic hibernation, several models of deficient humans were generated. Humans continued to degenerate through succeeding generations and interactions (breeding with other types of beings, primarily Martians).

Over the centuries, several early human hybrids on Earth were systematically annihilated and replaced with different models of hybridized humans. Most of the early strains of humans on Earth, vanished as did the history of planet Man, washed away with few remnants to be found.

The sun was much brighter and hotter during the era of Man. Planet Man's orbit around the sun provided Man with near perfect temperate and stable weather conditions. Mercury, Venus and Earth experienced hotter climates for that period of time. The whole of the star system was a hotter and a more suitable place for Reptilian and Serpent races, who thrived in hot environments.

The destruction of Man created violent meteor showers that befell the planet Earth every few years when the Earth moved into the path of the asteroid field that was created by planet Man's debris. Much of the surface of the Earth, at the time, was uninhabited by human equivalents (humanoids). Serpents and various renegade clans populated parts of Earth's surface and the interior spaces. Serpents and other reptilians also resided in submerged aquatic cities on the ocean floor, and in the endless caverns deep under the Earth's surface. Numerous other types of beings existed, and still do, inside and under Earth's crust, in the millions of miles of winding caves and tunnels. Some caves came about naturally through the flow of water; most were purposefully hollowed out by advanced races that came and went, throughout the ages of Earth.

During a time previous to the Ice Age, Neanderthals (and other semi-human variants), were at the mercy of asteroid storms that triggered horrific weather conditions on Earth. Massive tornado swarms, atrocious lightning discharges, and multiple enormous hurricanes lasting years battered Earth.

Storms were generated and fueled by the unrelenting meteor bombardment and the consequential volcanic eruptions triggered by natural and unnatural forces (some that were perpetrated by Serpents). Survival of the fittest, and the most determined creatures and beings, was part of the process to exterminate physically unfit beings from the stronger, more tolerant beings (beings designed for ceremonial games).

Barbaric rituals were instituted under the guise of training and brutal endurance tests, which were imposed on many of the early beings placed on Earth. Strategies towards humans and the offspring of Martians (Neanderthals) was a long, arduous process for those creatures destined to endure and flourish under horrific physical experiences. Serpents protected some of the "select" human tribes (those that fought the smartest to survive), providing for them and taking them to underground caverns during prearranged and extraordinary catastrophic events. Events that were scheduled periodically for the decimation of those left on the surface. Preferred breeds of recruits were taken on long journeys to distant planets within the star system where they received additional training and then returned back to Earth, as tribal leaders, priests, and warlords.

Planet Man was a treasure trove of enormous quantities of natural and manufactured resources. Mountains of gold and valleys of silver and an endless conglomeration of other precious metals were manufactured by humans, with the help of higher beings (and their mysterious machines). Humans made and wove precious metals into assortments of products, and in abundant quantities, and distributed the metals and other materials to all of its provinces in the star system.

Planet Man's iron core was substantially enormous and is the source of much of the iron meteorites that have showered down on Earth, and other planets and moons in the star system (during the multiple thousands of years after the destructions of Man). Gold and every metal that is known to modern-day humans spilled from the skies for eons after the destructions of Man. Most of the metals burned up inside of Earth's thick atmosphere, and released endless tons of elements into the clouds, and then into the oceans, seas, and land.

Cities whose buildings and streets were literally made of gold (for cosmic resonance as well as obscene opulence) sprouted up like mushrooms on Earth, prior to and after the Ice Age. Gold's superb electrical quantum properties made the precious metal ideal for technologically advanced beings and their lavish standards of living.

Renegades replicated high-tech marvels from their former places of origin, onto planet Earth, attempting to recreate what they had before they were vanquished and expelled to the lower regions of the galaxy.

Some of planet Man's gold that hadn't fallen to earth was harvested by Renegade beings from the debris that fell on the moon, Mars, Venus and Mercury, and that of which was drifting through space (the bulk). Salvaged gold was brought to Earth, for use in building powerful kingdoms and majestic "transitory" cities; cities that are now absent from Earth, and located in other places in this star system.

A selection of flora and fauna from planet Man was preserved in large space containers before the destruction of Man and relocated on Earth. Much of the existing flora and fauna on Earth, was killed off or removed as it was not complimentary to the new uses of planet Earth. Earth was designed to be a smaller and more diverse planet than planet Man.

Earth's populations are destined to leave a significantly reduced footprint in the star system, than did the humans of Man. Planet Man had a grander purpose, and roll, in the planetary system than what is planned for Earth. Much of Man's enormous footprint has since been erased by the Serpents. So as not to diminish or interfere with humanity's aspirations, to reach for the stars, for the sake of the superficial conquest of space "go where no man has gone before" (no such place exists in the would of the universe).

Planet Man and its moons were primarily populated by one race, a pure breed of human. In contrast, Earth would have several distinctive races of humans. Early Humans on Earth were subjected to cross pollination (breeding) by Martians, Reptilians, Serpents, and the hundreds of other breeds and races that were exiled from numerous star systems in the Milky Way.

Some exiled races found their way to Earth on their own, and some were brought to Earth by the gods or the agents of the gods. Thousands of races exist in the Milky Way, but only a fraction of the races are allowed to enter and pollinate within this star system, to cross-breed with Humans.

Pure breeds of humans (as those that were on planet Man) are abundant and common throughout the galaxy and the universe. Similarly, on other star systems, as happened in this star system, purebred humans are discontinued after they have served their cosmic and ecological reason for being. The pattern is not followed precisely in all similar planetary systems and can deviate drastically. Deviations generate far different outcomes, concerning the formation of physical and nonphysical entities. In this star system and others like it, humans are mated with dissimilar races to create unique products that are sustainable in the systems they are intended to function in. Many such variants of beings are destroyed soon after their purpose is resolved (finished).

Training and testing human combinations (hybrids) began as soon as humans were brought to Earth, from the staging areas located inside of massive cosmic container ships. Early humans were transported to Earth fully formed and ready to march. Some humans and hybrids had hibernating souls (functioned without souls) others that had no souls, received souls after they arrived on Earth. Memories were created and placed into the human minds, overriding old memories for those bodies that had a previous existence, and providing new memories in the mind for hybrids that had no previous memories. Souls processed whatever memories were uploaded into the mind with any latent memories that existed inside of the brain, and made that material their own.

Mazes for learning, survival and punishment, were created with timber, stones, and dirt. Sometimes humans had to help in the construction of multifaceted structures, laboring day and night to make the mazes that they would be tested in or sacrificed inside of. Design and construction of mazes and other structures were carried out by technologically advanced Renegades, and their robotic machines. Reptilians, androids, certain types of Greys, and other highly advanced biological and synthetic beings assisted or collaborated with Renegades, to create monolithic structures at several locations around the planet.

Having lost intellectual capacity (by the design of the Serpents), later humans were retrained in the intricacies of earthly existence and in the methods of subsistence. Hunting, capturing and domesticating animals, preserving food for the extended winter months, were a few of the lessons humans received. Fighting and defensive methods, and the construction of fortifications were employed, and leadership skills, developed and then hammered deep into the minds of the humans who were chosen to lead other humans into battles.

Human sacrifice and cannibalism were ritualistic lessons that humans had to endure under barbaric strategies that were instituted by Renegades. Humans were forced into aggressive, belligerent, activities by the Serpents, to help them cope, and survive against instinctively destructive beings that roamed on the surface of the Earth, and hid beneath the ground.

HUMAN ABDUCTIONS

Humans from Man were abducted and used at the inclination of Reptilian beings. Reptilians were never far from where humans lived, no matter the distance from planet Man. In addition to planet Man, and its moons, Reptilians could be found lurking in space cities in the far reaches of the star system and shadowing humans wherever humans congregated. Reptilians copulated with humans for pleasure, and to hybridize humans for uses and purposes within their own encampments. Reptilian races were many, and far-reaching, engulfing much of the star system during the time of Man. Reptilians took up residence on planets, moons and on large space-faring ships, to accommodate their planetary globe-trotting adventures.

Humans were not aware of their encounters, abductions, and exploits, done to them, by Reptilian beings. Reptilians placed humans under hypnotic spells before taking them to their bizarre ships, for activities, and then released them back to their normal lives, with memories wiped clean of the encounter. Man's humans were forever naïve of their manipulated lives and dual existences. Humans of that era lived pampered lives and had little to fear from the Reptilians or any other creatures (human lives were safe, more or less). Serpents protected humans (but not from the Reptilian's "harmless" exploits), up until they were directed to kill off the humans, and dismantle the human web that connected and stretched across the entire star system.

Reptilian beings invaded human societies and milked humans as if they were dairy cows. The pure breed of human genetic material served to replicate enzymes that were cultivated and stored by Reptilians. Reptilians used fresh-out-of-the-human-body gene material, for daily applications in reptilian enclaves. Reptilians could replicate human DNA but not the other elements that were above the biological, and that was associated with the living soul inside of humans. Reptilians had no access to human souls but souls affected human biology in ways that enhanced biological fundamentals that were essential to the Reptilians.

Reptilians are nomadic creatures, and travel in ships through space, in a perpetual migratory route, which takes them to every location in the star system. Reptilians swim through space, like pods of whales traversing a cosmic ocean. Reptilians serve multiple purposes for themselves and for the higher beings (gods). Purposes of which "most" remain ambiguous, and the rest, only known by the gods, who secretly employed the Reptilians.

Some breeds of Reptilians are antagonistic to the Serpents. Serpents are superior to most Reptilian beings, even though they share similar traits, genes, and functions, in the broad reptilian family of creatures. Serpents are the most recent and current overlords of the inner planets, in this star system, placing them over, and consequently, at odds with some of their less respected, reptilian brothers.

Abducted humans from Man, and Man's territories, were taken aboard Reptilian ships, and hooked up to biological machinery, and tapped like kegs of beer. Blood and other biological materials were siphoned from human bodies and inserted into the bodies of human clones, for later use by Reptilians. Clones were created from the DNA of the abducted human, from which the siphoned material was later stored inside of. DNA used for cloning was harvested from humans when they were only weeks old, and at their purest biological state.

Human clones were kept alive inside of individualized cells (compartments) that lined the outer walls of Reptilian ships. Clones were generally free of souls and were only used as biological containers, keeping the soul-influenced-fluids taken from abductees, fresh for prolonged interstellar journeys.

After taking fluids from the humans, Reptilians injected hormones into the lymphatic system of the abducted humans, and the humans were released and returned to the place of abduction.

Not all Man humans were abducted. How or why any human was chosen and placed into the program by the Reptilians remains a mystery. The frequency of abductions depended on factors of convenience and the availability of marked humans. Dynamics concerning when Reptilians happened to be in the same area with subjected humans, was one of the factors.

Reptilians that broke protocol or violated rules of engagement with humans (set by the Serpents) were hunted and killed by Serpents or their bounty hunters. Such actions ended the abductions of humans associated with those Reptilians. The humans were then free from further abductions by other Reptilians.

Occasionally, abducted humans were compromised (killed) if they happened to be in the possession of the Reptilians during the discovery and subsequent execution of the rogue Reptilian clans. Depending on the situation, and its potential volatility, the rescue of humans, was not always a desirable option.

In addition to infusing abducted humans with hormones, and other biological agents, Reptilians tagged humans, branded them as the property belonging to a certain Reptilian clan. Tagging humans were not done for tracking purposes but to let other Reptilians know who that human belonged to. Reptilian clans had their own unique trademarks, which were mostly honored by other Reptilian clans.

During the time of Man, Reptilians were not challenged or confronted by Renegades, concerning human abductions. Renegades typically shied away from Reptilian affairs, and their presumed property (preferred not to tangle with them). In principle, the Reptilians provided a valuable measure of protection to the humans, in the abduction program, by providing another layer of defense to the humans.

Serpents were not aggressive towards other races of Reptilians, unless or until the Reptilians crossed into restricted zones, and violated protocol governing planets and moons. Protocol (things allowed), varied markedly and was determined by circumstances and types of beings and creatures that existed within the sphere of each planetary system in the system. For instance, humans received more protections than did Martians and other more aggressive type beings. Otherwise, there would be far fewer humans left to pick through for the numerous and ongoing breeding programs in the star system.

Serpents had significant reserves of soulless human bodies in quarantine, hidden on ships that traveled to and fro throughout the star system, enough to sustain future Serpent projects and objectives. Container ships storing humans were under constant guard and were moved around as in a shell game, to keep Renegades, and Reptilians, from discovering and capturing the containers filled with human bodies.

Some Renegade tribes vehemently opposed being mated with humans, and attacked and killed all humans they encountered, often tracking humans down, wherever they believed humans might be found (in the star system). They also killed off their own kind that had been mixed with humans, by the Serpents.

MUMMIES

Mummification (what appeared to be mummifications) was used to store and transport Humans and Martians to various locations in the star system. Such practices triggered copycat mummification attempts by various human tribes/societies who had observed the strange practices performed by the gods, and then attempted to mimic the behavior of the "gods" by wrapping the deceased (for later reanimation).

When transported to Earth, some humans and Martians were brought back to life "ritualistically" by Serpent priests. It was a practice made to appear as if the priests had god-like powers, to bring back the dead and give them renewed life. Which the Serpents did, and do have, to a certain extent; when the Serpents were allowed the privilege (power of life and death) by spiritualized beings, who regularly pop souls into meat-sacks for the Serpents.

Humans and Martians were and are transported to Earth in huge cylinder ships that hover in the sky; and in olden times, were visible to the awe-struck natives, who were often corralled near the Serpent-built temples, and allowed to watch and be witnesses to the "miracles" performed by the "gods."

Humans and Martians, fresh off the celestial ships of the gods, came individually wrapped, encased in a jell-like substance, and sealed under a transparent, rubbery material that protected the bodies during extended periods of storage in space. Ceremonies, sometimes lasting for days, marked the resurrections of numerous humanoids that would eventually be mated with multitudes of races.

Martian and human bodies, were released into new environments, primarily Earth, under the direction of Serpent ministers and priests. Once the bodies were ceremoniously unwrapped, souls were placed inside of them by higher beings, not the Serpents or the gods, but other beings that showed up for the occasion. Locals didn't know about or see the higher spirit beings and credited the gods (often Serpents) for the miracles. Once souls entered the bodies, the bodies jumped to life and were taken to other ceremonial places, usually underground (earlier times) and then to pyramid structures, for further processing, pre and post-Ice Age eras.

Millions of cocooned Human, Martian, and Renegade hybrids (human equivalents) were and are encased (individually) and stored inside of ships. The cocoons are adrift in space, inside the ships, and in a state of infinite preservation. Some of the preserved bodies contain souls; most are empty containers, carcasses that serve as repositories of oodles of varieties of chromosomes, and other biological material, some that dates back to early star system societies. Material that will again see daylight, during multiple and prearranged future times, when batches of beings will be reanimated, with some of that material, and released onto planets. Primarily Earth.

Humans and every kind of being, flora, and fauna, insects, fish and microbes that set foot in this star system that existed millions and billions of years ago, are stored for eternity inside of ships adrift in space. DNA and other biological material, encompassing every period of biological life, in this star system, is readily available in millions of such ships (available to the gods and Serpents). Such materials will outlast the death of the star, and the planetary system, and will be conserved by the gods, who at the appointed time will seal the containers and placed them into one of the endless billions of galactic halls (massive space structures) dispersed near the center of the galaxy.

Several early human societies, with the help of Serpent priests, mummified humans, animals, and other creatures and buried them in the ground or in motif-rich ornate tombs. Often only for appearance sake, for the ceremonial indulgences of the people in those communities. Many mysterious looking beings were supposedly mummified and placed into burial chambers, but instead were taken aboard ships and their bodies stored away, forever hidden from modern humans.

Mummies served purposes for the gods and the Serpents, who accessed the reservoirs of biological material for future times, whether the corpses were stored on ships or buried on planets and moons. Unknown to the humans and other beings, that were involved in the ceremonies (caretakers, laborers, even some of the priests) many mummies were transported to other planets and moons in the star system, and to other star systems in the galaxy, and sometimes reanimated. Occasionally the revived body received the same soul it had before it died, but more often it received a temporary proxy soul, and sometimes no soul at all.

Such beings have been placed into storage, hidden in secret places on planets, and moons, inside of pyramids, within solid blocks of granite, for safe keeping. Until a time when they will be called upon, by the Serpents, and released.

LARGE WINGED BEINGS

During the time of Man, large winged beings ferried individual humans to mysterious subterranean places on planet Man. The creatures remained unidentified and did not belong to the Serpent or other Reptilian races. Serpents are an advanced strand of one of the many Reptilian races in the star system. The mysterious winged beings were an unknown anomaly even for the highly advanced Serpents. The winged beings are not renegades, as are many of the creatures existing in low-level star systems.

Winged beings didn't use ships and ferried humans inside of pouches or strange types of containers. The winged beings had the bodies of humans with the heads of birds, lions, monkeys, humans or any number of other types of creatures. The beings communicated telepathically with the humans in the universal language, the same language spoken by the humans on Man. Winged beings moved through dimensions as well as the physical realms. The beings are invisible to all but the humans or whoever or whatever creatures they make contact with.

After the winged beings had taken the human (usually while sleeping), the humans became one with the creatures. Where the beings took their captives or why is perplexing, more so for those that were seized, and their lives dramatically changed soon after. Changed humans were an anomaly for the Serpents and even the gods. Abnormalities that afflicted humans from Man were watched closely. Some of the humans afflicted received additional scrutiny and were quarantined away from the herd, by the Serpents. Most of the quarantined humans were never seen again.

Humans were seldom aware that they were taken by numerous creatures of the night, and always during nighttime. Gods and Serpents knew; who, why and what, most of the time, and as shepherds, dealt with situations as they deemed fitting for each situation. Usually staying within the parameters that were put in place by the higher beings, governing the galaxy, and abiding by them, but not always.

Humans of Man dreamt during sleep, as do modern humans and other creatures. Within dreams exists realities of places that are kept hidden from the cognizant mind of humans. Realities of past existences and lives are inherent inside of all dreams, regardless whether the dreamer is man or beast. Beasts from the animal kingdom could have been human or any number of other type creatures existing in the galaxy, in their previous lives. Dreams are places more real than the fabricated illusions most three-dimensional beings find themselves wrapped inside of.

Inside of dreams humans and animals can visit with family and friends on the other side of life, in real time or some other time; past, present and future. Often the visit from a visitor(s) is from a past reality on some other planetary system, skewed, fragmented and confusing because it is viewed in a higher dimension than the dimension where the dreamer exists in. Sometimes the dream shows a future place and situation that the soul will encounter in its next incarnation. In some dreams, the human or animal is allowed to feel and experience the pain or happiness that they have brought about in other humans or in other creatures, creatures, and animals with vestiges of souls within them.

The dream-world is a multifaceted region that bridges higher and lower dimensions, in the body and mind, and can be in a place that exists externally and away from the physical realms. Dreams are a teaching tool used by higher beings, and a place of nightmares, where lower beings can set up torment chambers inside of people's minds. Lower beings are a loose cadre of lost and tormented souls. Entities that also include the ghosts of past enemies, attempting to take revenge on a soul they believed wronged them, in some way, in some previous existence.

Several categories of winged beings exist, some without the wings and some without souls. Similarities that fused them into their unique category was their placidness and swiftness. Rapid movement many times that of hummingbird wings (wingless or winged) propelled the beings through dimensional space (rapid body movement, not the wings, propelled them). The beings became invisible during most of their travels only becoming visible to the much slower humans when they decelerated (entered lower dimensional space), for the purpose of interacting in the three-dimensional realm (briefly), where humans and Martians are detained.

Soulless creatures, mechanical in nature, like physical living machinery, buzzed around the winged and wingless beings and served an unknown purpose to them (unknown to the casual observer, who would be paralyzed with terror at such a sight). Most supernatural beings had bizarre entourages, and followings that were unique to each being, which followed them everywhere. Such paraphernalia operated independently or in conjunction with other paraphernalia (gadgets), which created situations conjure by the being (owner of the gadgets).

Serpents, Reptilians, and some Renegades have similar abilities to cloak, morph and move through dimensions (with or without attending gadgets), which gives them advantages over humans, Martians and a few other similarly classed beings.

MARS BEFORE THE LAST WAR

Just as other planets in the star system, Mars had hundreds of periods/stages (ages) of beings, animals, insects and plant life that transitioned in and out of existence. During the later stages of Martian existence, prior to subjugation by the Serpents, Martians existed in a state of conflict fraught with warring Martian clans. Hostilities among Martian clans, and between other races of beings, on other planets, spanned millions of years. Mars never experienced an age of peace and spread their unique form of warfare to Earth.

Martians' innate aggressions served a useful purpose for the Serpents, who funneled Martian clans to various places, including Earth. Serpents turned Martians loose to hunt and desecrate undesirable spawn from indigenous beings and creature-infestations, associated with Renegade beings. Earth received countless Martian clans that chewed and clawed their way through many societies during gruesome periods on Earth. Some early societies were completely wiped away; others were assimilated and became part of the Martian bands. Which in turn, spawned other types of barbaric beings that roamed the lands on Earth, for centuries, prior to the last Ice Age. Spawn that would itself need cleansing by future generations of other more vicious beings. Renegade, Martian, and human hybrids, flooded the earth, and again were decimated, most destroyed by floods, pestilences, plagues and other calamities created or aided by the Serpents.

Martians came in many shapes and sizes, large, tall, small, short, hairy and apelike, to mention only a few variations. Martians, as it true with many physical life forms in the Milky Way, are a conglomeration of species and races of beings from other star systems.

Some races on Mars, as well as other planets, are indigenous to the planets they were created on, concerning genetic material and other elements of their physical makeup. Martians, Humans, Serpents, Reptilians, and Renegades, in all their multiples of representations (hybrids and races), are not unique in the galaxy or the universe. Similar races exist in and on millions of other planets and moons throughout the Milky Way system.

Likewise, there are millions of star systems that have unique, bizarre, and very strange beings and civilizations on them. Billions of such places, and strangely unique to each other, which don't compare in any way to the beings and creatures residing in this star system.

This star system is home to numerous bizarre beings and creatures of which only a few are mentioned in this book. There are billions of insects from the microscopic to several inches long on this planet alone. And that's the range of "intelligent" life forms and beings in existence in this star system, with the vast majority of creatures and beings invisible and unknown to humans.

Martians had communities within cities and functioned under various forms of laws that were imposed on various clans, which dictated rules specific to species and race of Martians. Mars was a hodgepodge of races congealed from millions of years of Martian conquest on various planets and moons, and the amalgamation and mating with subjugated races. Over the period of thousands of hybridized generations, emerged a social order, a type of civilization (of sorts) of Martians.

Mars was a war planet, and they had a substantial military presence in other planetary systems and moons in the star system. Martians had attempted to colonize Earth but only managed to install a few settlements for short durations before succumbing to Reptilian and Serpent attacks, who also had ambitions for planet Earth.

Martian technology was substantial and helped carry them to the outer reaches of the star system, and beyond. How far beyond even the Martians were never sure about. Traveling out of the star system without the aid of higher beings was suicide, but Martians entered the dark vastness between the stars nonetheless.

Martians found refuge on planets, moons, and large asteroids that were outside the star system, and deep into the dark abyss of endless space. Some Martians, in their search for real estate, became victims of beastly and foreboding creatures. Infinite types of entities, beings and creatures, prowl in the cold oblivion of intergalactic space. Unimaginable numbers of planets and planetoids exist in the colossal vastness of space, which acts as harbors for inestimable numbers of interesting creatures. It is a cosmic soup that galactic stars bathed in. And from where bizarre monsters feed on whatever organic material lands on their not-so-barren rocks.

Darkness was broken in places with light from failed dwarf stars and from planets that gave off luminosity from internal heat. Other sources of light are generated by the advanced lifeforms inhabiting the planets, moons and asteroids existing between star systems.

Martians had families or a semblance of what a family is (a group of beings under one roof but not necessarily related). Mars had large cities and small villages with cooperatives, associations and joint agreements with other villages, cities, and towns. Martians were not separated or differentiated by countries as Earth is today, it was a conglomeration of cities large and small, fortified and widely spread out. The planet was ruled by a council of powerful Martians, who attempted to rule over Mars and its many subsidiaries that were distributed on various planets and moons in the system (and bring a semblance of order to them). But order was a misnomer, and only wishful thinking, on a planet that was run by belligerent warlords. Warlords had absolute power (more or less, mostly less) over their domains, and sometimes shared power with other warlords, over larger territories on Mars, and the territories that were off planet.

Pockets of peace and tranquility existed on Mars, briefly, seldom persisting for long. Skirmishes between warlords were often settled after short encounters, to avoid prolonged hostilities from which war-weary Martians didn't have the resources to maintain for extended periods. Subsequently, it was the lack of resources that allowed for episodes of peace, between otherwise blood-thirsty warring factions.

Martian societies were deeply involved with the occults. Conjuring with the spirit worlds and placing spells on each other for fun or revenge. Unlike modern times on Earth, the spirits were openly active and frequently manifested around Martian clans. And gleefully sharing power and knowledge of the intricacies of incantations with their Martian hosts. Spells had a real punch to them, and Martian wizards could turn other Martians into freakish creatures, with the help of dark entities that administered potent drugs and potions to the victims. The calling into the open (summoning) dark spirits to fight against enemies, was prevalent, which afflicted foes for short periods or forever, depending on the spells cast on them.

A few overlords attempted to control some types of paranormal activity, and expelled sorcerers from kingdoms that had fallen into morasses of treachery, and killed off some of those who continued to practice the dark arts aggressively.

Black magic owned Martian societies and manifested within their blood and souls. Belief in benevolent beings was a strange concept and one that was never taken seriously by most Martians.

Martian landscape had places of ruins from civilizations past. Many layers of ruins existed underneath large modern cities and remained in use by vagabond Martians. Many types of Martian beings existed on Mars, few of which survived the Serpent cleansing. Martians experimented and bred with many types of beings, creatures, and animals. Most of the breeding activity was fruitless. An activity that succeeded was turned loose and left to survive on its own or die if it wasn't discovered and destroyed by clan leaders first. Breeding with animals was not condoned by the primary Martian leadership but was left to local tribe leaders to control the doings of their clans.

Martians were a technologically advanced race. Having received technological assistance in exchange for their cooperation with Renegade beings, throughout much of Mar's colorful and violent, history. Martians were capable of cloaking themselves and also cloaking their entire ships. Their bag of tricks included chameleon technology, where they ingested pills that pigmented their skin, allowing them to blend into their surroundings far better than any chameleon, and enabling them to avoid detection. Employing such skills made finding Martians a challenge for other Martians, and sometimes for the Serpents.

Modern Martians on Mars, those that were allowed to survive Serpent eradication, and those that escaped the Serpents by hiding out in deep space, or inside niches and crannies on Mars, or on the other planets, moons, comets, and meteors, had their cloaking and chameleon capabilities, to thank.

All technologically advanced beings in the star system have the ability to conceal themselves (on some level). A technology that modern humans on Earth have only recently and officially, "discovered" (gifts from the gods). Military and other covert organizations operating on Earth, had received that technology much earlier.

POLTERGEIST

Serpents destroyed many Martian clans due to their extensive paranormal aberrations, which manifested into physical mutations. And in some instances had turned clans into infectious, leprous, outcasts, within Martian societies.

Serpents, gods, and Reptilians had paranormal clients that they engaged with in daily affairs, but the clients were not controlled by the dark and magical creatures as some Martians were. Martians had a long-standing affair with spirit beings, and that opened up a vast network of paranormal vortexes into Martian territories. Martians infested portions of planet Man with their paranormal critters. Critters that infiltrated and mated with some of Man's humans. Reptilians exterminated the Martians, the critters, and the infected humans, soon after they were detected.

Reptilians rooting out contaminated humans was a service to the Serpents, whose job it was to keep the human flock free of external tampering (except for Reptilian tampering, which was allowed and part of the program for the Humans on Man).

Paranormal creatures and beings created havoc and mischief in the Martian communities, wherever dark spirits dominated. It was a Pandora's Box, for the Martians, they opened a vortex between dimensions, and released a massive ghoul contagion on Mars.

The contagion was a consequence and a paradox created by the destruction of millions of Martians, by the Serpents. The nature of Martian souls (lacking in purity) didn't allow for them to be appropriately absorbed into hades (a staging area for errant souls), and many souls lingered and pestered the living Martians, who had opened themselves up to dark forces. As happens in a debilitated immune system, the constant annoyance by the ghosts garnered the ghouls' access into the physical realms of the feeble, Martian souls.

Subsequently, Martian tribes and clans brought with them their black magic, incantations, and rituals, to Earth, eons before they would be mated to modern Humans pre-Ice Age, but also post Ice Age barbarians. Magic itself is neither good nor bad, but in the hands of mortals, it becomes the extension of the souls who wield it.

Paranormal creatures were allowed by some Martian clans to enter into their bodies and be possessed as a group. And the paranormal creatures ended up owning the bodies they enter into. Taking hostage the original souls occupying Martian bodies. Martians possessed mediocre souls to begin with and were easily led to do the bidding of dark creatures.

Poltergeists are remnants of lost souls trapped on planets, moons and in space, wherever soul-bearing beings reside (the past and present). Poltergeists have no fixed form and are horrifically disfigured creatures, having lost significant soul mass (energy) to keep them whole and tolerable, rather than appalling and frightening to be around.

Poltergeist can only possess beings that allow them entry into their lives; they have to be asked in to get in. Poltergeist promises the moon and other delights to the enfeebled souls (residing inside of physical bodies), in exchange for a physical body to rest inside of. But rest eludes both the poltergeist and the foolish host. The host is terrorized and paralyzed, while the poltergeist takes control and manifests powers and magic that is attributed to the person or being that is possessed. Poltergeists deceive others into believing they are the person that they have taken over, by using similar speech patterns and mannerisms of the hostage soul.

Once infested by menacing spirits, the Martian was doomed, and nothing but the death of the body would release the Martian from the dark spirit(s), and the treacherous influences they brought with them.

Contemporary humans have a different type of soul than what the Martians had in the past. The brand of soul Humans are endowed with, is less likely to fall victim to poltergeists as the kind that infested Martians. Still, some humans manage to be enticed and become prey to dark spirits, who will torment and further obfuscate their lives, without possessing them.

Humans are more prone to follow mesmerizing leaders whose souls are from the phantom realms. When that happens, whole nations of people are condemned to endure the designs of the one physical dark spirit or spirits, and a nation might have to perish to be rid of their ideologically deranged slave master(s).

Frequent conflicts have been initiated and fought by dark forces that had penetrated and mesmerized Martian clans. Whole villages and nations, on Mars, and on Earth have been drawn into physical and maniacal combat between peoples, which were initiated by entities with roots in the phantom zone.

The spirit world and all of its realms is far larger and grander than the physical world, and has always influenced and interfered with souls existing in the mucked-up physical planetary spheres. The spectrum of levels in the spirit world runs the gamut from the lowest points of hades to the astronomical heights of nirvana. From the spirit spectrums are where battles for souls is the most intense and an interminable affair. All souls will ultimately return to the spirit domain and align with the forces of their choosing.

Martian souls believed (knew) that they were destined to move to lower levels of existence (hades) after death. A concept they brought with them to Earth, and which survived in human communities that they had infiltrated and assimilated into over the centuries.

Martians had souls of a strain forged by beings from Red Dwarf stars, (stars that had yet to go yellow). Such beings deposited their spawn (souls) on planetary systems with yellow suns, to mature on. Many types of strains of souls come from massive star clusters, where stars are in full bloom, near the center of the Milky Way galaxy. Many more types of soul strains originate from other types of star systems, newer and smaller stars, which have not yet ripened and stabilized. Such souls are forged in hotter furnaces and undergo additional torments during their extensive and drawn out existences.

Modern human souls are tinged with a mixture of Martian, Reptilian, and Renegade, soul essence. Humans on Earth are a hodgepodge of souls with varying flavors of highly dissimilar beings while inhabiting similar genetically constructed "human" bodies. But similarities end there. Human souls have a mixture of the spirit-tags from the above beings. Which tags any one human carries or which tag dominates, determines place and race on Earth, and possibly, where they go from here.

Modern human bodies are far different than the bodies of the beings that originally spawned them. Bodies on Earth are specifically designed and tuned for Earth-type planets (during this era) and the diversity of souls fated to inhabit them. Human bodies continue to undergo modifications to accommodate new situations. Many different types of souls are scheduled to come to Earth in the near future. Gene mutations specifically designed for the corporal containers of the new arrivals are already happening in the bodies of their future bloodlines.

REPTILIANS

Non-human elements (Reptilians) were symbiotic with the humans of Man. Reptilians existed among the humans while remaining unknown, unseen, and concealed to the humans (as a worm inside of an apple. The demise of humans drastically reduced the numbers of Reptilians that were dependent on human populations for their far-reaching and elusive enterprises in the star system.

Pure-bred Humans from the planet Man made up the largest population of beings in the star system. Humans existed on every planet, moon, large and small asteroids, and the millions of space cities dispersed in every nook and cranny in the star system, out to its very edge. This overabundance of humans was favorable to the parasitic Reptilians, who also were spread out all over the star system (wherever humans were they were).

Reptilians are far more advanced than their Man-human hosts, and modern humans too. Reptilians are extremely illusive creatures, even amongst themselves. Humans were unaware that Reptilians had an insatiable need for human bile and other organic substances only found inside the human biological machine (due to soul-element properties).

Reptilians, like bedbugs, came to the humans during the night, while the humans slept and dreamt. Reptilians immobilized humans with their minds and approached them from behind. Reptilians sometimes laid next to the human and inserted a syringe-like tentacle into the back or side of the human while the humans slept in their own beds. Most contacts with humans happened where the humans lived and not on board Reptilian ships (during certain epochs). Reptilian tentacles or other appendages found their own way to human organs: spleen, liver, intestines, pancreas, gallbladder, kidneys, appendix, liver, brain and any other body parts of interest to the Reptilian creatures. After insertion, measured amounts of liquids were siphoned from the organs.

If it was the first contact with a human, Reptilians inserted a permanent tap, onto each individual body part that needed a tap. Taps were used during future encounters, minimizing irritation to the body organs. Contact was periodic and by the same Reptilian during the course of that human's life. The exchange of bodily fluids was beneficial to both humans and Reptilians.

Humans of Man had a unique relationship with
Reptilians that did not translate to similar encounters with other
types of Reptilian dealings, occurring with Martians and modern
humans on Earth; who experience far different encounters and
realities with Reptilians of the modern era.

Serpent overlords exterminated certain types of Reptilian elements and societies wherever they discovered them (a process continued to this day). Not all Reptilian races carried the mammalian genome within their reptilian bodies and had no allowable claim to humans and their biological materials. Reptilians are repositories of multitudes of genomes for an assortment of animals, insects and plant life, in existence throughout the star system.

Reptilian beings serve multiple purposes inside of star systems. And some of those purposes benefit different non-Reptilian races of beings and therefore are tolerated by the gods. When a purpose is deemed dubious and found to be counterproductive or fraudulent, by the gods, the gods dispatch Serpents to determine the type and race of the Reptilians in question and deal with them accordingly.

Reptilians have adapted to the various revisions and variations of humans on Earth, for untold millenniums, after the demise of planet Man, and their own reduction in numbers due to Man's demise. The new and ever-changing dynamics of human breeds have challenged the surviving Reptilian clans that are determined to keep a human connection to supplement their own existence, and relevance, in the star system.

It's a human/Reptilian connection and a conundrum (awkward on many levels especially in modern humans), but an association that is sanctioned by higher elements in the galactic realm (a realm that is far above the star system gods).

This ever-present sphere of powerful beings (those above the gods) that infringes on the physical universe from a nonphysical dominion, and institutes matters that remain far reaching and beyond 3-dimensional concepts and understanding, are beyond approach. They are entities of a power base that's as ambiguous as it is secret in its dealings in the affairs of humans, and those too numerous to mention, beings that interact and cross paths with humans.

Many Reptilian races are not highly progressed spiritually or technologically (yet far more so than humans are). They are provided (allowed) limited technology, enough to carry out specific assigned duties on lower planets, by the gods that rule over star systems.

GODS OF THE STAR SYSTEM

Gods of the star system resided wherever they wished but congregate mostly in and around Saturn, Jupiter, Uranus, and numerous space-platforms orbiting near the sun. The gods have physical bodies and enjoy the pleasures of the flesh, as do humans, Martians, Serpents, Reptilians and numerous other intelligent beings incorporated into biological bodies.

Food, wine, and sex are universal amusements pursued in the physical, albeit, illusionary realms. Illusionary for mere mortals, that is. The gods created their own bodies and are at the apex of physical perfection. Or as near perfection as is possible to achieve in the lower realms of corporal existence, even for the gods.

Gods have no limit to physical appearances, and take on many forms to interface and blend in with subordinate beings. Physical appearance depends on the beings they visit with or have dealings with. Fleshy, synthetic and mechanical costumes morph onto the gods at their command, to suit any and all situations.

Aging and other anomalies do not afflict the gods. Such anomalies are plagues gods themselves regularly subject humans, Martians, and other mortals. Subordinate beings (mortals), living in physical form and lacking the technological advantages available only to the gods, and their designees, bear the brunt of the despairing inconsistencies of lower level existence.

The gods are not gods in the true sense of the word, or understanding of what a god is (omnipotent being). The gods are gods in the capacity to create and administer to the physical beings (containers) that are indigenous to this star system, and those handpicked and brought here by the gods themselves, from other star systems and places. Gods are not the creators of matter but are manipulators of biological material and elements to the extent allowed them by superior higher beings, those beings ruling larger portions of the galactic nurseries above the mere star system gods.

Gods have the authority to expel or exterminate non-indigenous beings which permeate into this star system from other star systems, and from the vastness of space existing between star systems. Gods hold the keys to the gates of this star system and control (more or less) who or what can come and go concerning the "physical" realms. The nonphysical (ethereal) realms are administered by beings of a higher caliber than the local star gods. The larger-than-life Super Beings operate from mysterious supernatural realms somewhere in the cosmic dimensions.

Higher spiritualized beings don't concern themselves with matters of the flesh, and all of its elusive trappings enticing the amorphous souls and act only to give an account of soul progression in whatever realms of physicality souls are placed into, by them.

The gods (because they were known as such by early humans), didn't always rule from a distance but were and are hands on, and often set up shop on the inner planets in the star system, to manage juvenile creations. Gods lived among the beings that they produced or procured from distant star enterprises. The gods designed the cities and architecture for villages, towns, and cities, to suit the unique needs and requirements of individual tribal groups and larger civilizations.

Gods fashioned the cultures they desired to create for themselves and for their creatures (mortals), during any particular eras of exploits on Mars, Earth, and on other planets and moons. Taking physicalized souls on wild and fanciful journeys of the gods' choosing was a high privilege for those picked to come along. Journeys with the gods are wicked trials that run the gamut from the heights of ecstasy to the depths of soul despair and degradation.

Serpents and other types of Reptilians, and various clans of Renegades, also created villages, cities and classes of races that were their own hybridized offspring, to do with as they saw fit. It was a breed of spawn that often clashed with humanoid tribes and Martian clans, and in the mix created other types of beings.

The gods lived lavish lives as gods in whatever hellhole they descended into or created. Bringing comforts and lifestyles to the most treacherous of places on every planet and moon in their domain (mostly for themselves). Ships of the gods were havens of superb luxury and magic for the lucky few human and Martian chieftains (and other type beings) brought into the exclusive fold, for learning and for the bewilderment of the chosen mortals.

Gods usually ended their stints and their dominions of population centers with a bang. Destroying much or all of their earthly belongings and creations, and making it appear as if the civilization was conquered by marauding bands from nearby or by other more powerful civilizations in the region. As in the case with the Etruscans, who made it look as if they were destroyed by their apprentices, the Romans, and leaving little if any evidence of their true nature, and purpose, to be discovered by future generations of mortals. Many civilizations vanished without a trace hundreds of thousands of years ago, as have some that vanish recently, in the last few thousand years or less, due to similar exterminations by the gods that created them.

Civilizations don't vanish; they are vanquished or moved off the planet, and taken elsewhere, or destroyed completely or made to assimilate with existing civilizations in the area or with emerging ones.

Ships of the gods are the size they need to be to accommodate whole populations and cities of beings; populations that numbered in the thousands or in the millions of beings. Human and Martian populations were transitioned and transported between planets for new settlements or additions to existing settlements, periodically.

Selected human leaders were allowed privileges of knowing certain facets and aspects of the Alien overlords and their designs on human populations. Recruits received inside, and insightful information on a number of programs humans and Martians had to undergo.

Benefits enjoyed by the lucky few mortals were extravagant voyages to other planets and moons in the star system. That were given as part of the preparation for their eventual privileged positions, as the sons and daughters of the gods (which they were allowed to boast about). Chosen humans or other type beings were often mortals and only fed enough information to allow them to demand respect and obedience from their subjects (mostly humans) for a prescribed time. Such mortal leaders put in place by the gods, received little in the way of having accurate knowledge about the true nature of the universe, and the facts concerning the infestation of planets by multiple layers of physical and spiritual beings.

The gods held near absolute power but not absolute power in the star system. Gods were repeatedly challenged by forces that roamed the galaxy, and whose allegiances were ambiguous and hostile towards the gods, and the creatures under the dominium of the gods.

The gods ranked above the Serpents, and the various other Reptilian beings, who mostly worked under the directions and willfulness of the gods. Insubordinate Reptilian clans regularly challenged the powers and authority of the "god-forsaken" regions and sectors of the star system, where the gods tended to avoid for nebulous aims and reasons.

Battles between the gods and rebellious Reptilians were and are fierce and often result in the destruction or ejection of Reptilians from planets, moons and sometimes from the star system. Occasionally, the gods suffer setbacks and defeat by powerful races of beings; unknown beings that stray into the galaxy and into the star system from beyond the peripheries (mysterious regions) that reside in the massively extensive and endless space between galactic fortresses (galaxies).

Gods do not reproduce (give birth to other gods), and have no family structure or race, while occupying "temporary" positions as godly beings. Gods coexist in large cities inside of planets and moons and on the thousands of enormous starships that orbit so-called gas giant planets, and the ships that constantly patrol and move about the star system. Gods and their ships can leave the star system and travel to most places in the galaxy, for duties or for the leisure of the trip. Gods cannot leave the galaxy; while under the commitment of performing duties in appointed star systems (as can higher spiritualized beings, the occasional advisers to the gods).

Advisers have immense freedoms and access to the whole of multiple universes, and the infinite dimensions above the physical realms. They are Supreme Beings but are not the epitome, the apex that exists at the stratum of super beings.

Star gods live exquisite and utopic lives, never wanting nor needing anything. However, the gods must remain dutiful and engage with humans and other beings on some level as part of their responsibilities. Entry-level gods volunteer their time and can incarnate on Earth or other planets and moons as members of the race of beings they endear to work with. Some gods-in-training, know and are aware of their missions while humans or other creature types. A few of the freshmen gods are not fully aware of their mission while the mission is in progress until the mission is accomplished.

Gods come into existence by being placed into fully formed bodies of their choosing. Gods are souls that have advanced from rigorous realities as is found on Earth and have progressed to utopic-level planets, and from other types of realities. From utopia, souls can choose to become gods of star systems or move up to higher positions in the galactic province. Gods have broken the cycle of reincarnation imposed on the sliver of the spectrum, where souls that were assigned to this corner of the galaxy are carved from. Gods are free to choose to reincarnate to a grander range of life forms existing in the galaxy, to fulfill specific duties, physical desires or for any reason they wish.

Gods revel in all the perks available to them in the physical realms. Living in exquisite palatial kingdoms with multitudes of servants and administrators, obediently fulfilling their every need and want. Gods have headquarters and arrangements on large estates on every planet, every moon, and on multitudes of colossal spaceships, fleets of them, which are much more than humble abodes. Gods enjoy the lavish and extravagant cuisine and sip on the wines pressed from the sweet grapes of wrath, for wrath is what the gods do best.

Male gods sport handsome physiques and are adorned with superb personality and fluid speech. Female gods flaunt gorgeously and tantalizingly figures, complemented with exquisite dispositions and elegance. Gods morphed into any form, being or creature, they wish or desire. Gods are the masters of all personalities and are wickedly shrewd, and graciously benevolent, and everything in between.

Gods enjoyed mixing it up at gatherings and festivities with the other gods in their kingdoms. Gods are the original party animals. The gods display human characteristics to a tee, the good, the bad and the ugly, of characteristics; for fun and pleasure or for purely business dealings with lesser beings.

The gods act egotistical and gluttonous when they are in the council of human chieftains, leaders, priests, and shamans, as part of their performances (acts) to blend in with the mortals.

Gods are literally paternal and maternal with humans, sowing and spawning new beings and fostering them within human populations of their own making and design.

Gods create humans in their own image, a biblical passage that is literal, compared to most passages which are allegorical. Modern humans mistakenly believe that the gods are omnipotent and above the carnal addictions plaguing mere mortals. However, the gods are a perfect version of the human image, physically, sexually and adhere to numerous other carnal desires, even if and when they are only acting.

Gods don't marry each other nor are they monogamous. Instead, they frolic freely with other gods and humans too. Gods enjoy the companionship of other gods as well as all the creatures they encounter or create.

Living spaces of the gods are opulent and spacious with numerous mysteriously magical rooms inside. Some rooms are configured and dedicated to items of interest and intrigue to the individual and distinctive tastes of each god.

Gods are physical beings, and they enjoy physical things. Architecture, art, nature, and any number of items that brings pleasure to sentient beings. Gods lived as mortals in previous lives and have collected items during such lifetimes. Gods have placed vestiges of such items they admired most into their collections. Reclaiming original things and replacing them with perfect replicas (or nothing at all), and display the items with their vast collection of physical mementos (from past life experiences).

"Sam, you are pulling my leg right? Why in hell would gods care about the junk they once owned in a past life?" "Are we talking about the all-powerful (more or less) gods that are at the helm of star systems, or snotty-nosed nostalgic-crazed humans?"

Sam's reply, "Snotty-nosed humans, tend to hold on to past sentimental memories with physical objects. Gods come from many races, have lived multiple lives, and some lives hold pleasant memories of people/beings they have loved (children, lovers, dear friends and memorable situations). Such emotions and conditions leave imprints on physical objects. Physical objects can be collected; loved ones can move on to other realities that are not reachable by the gods, while they preside over star systems."

Gods enjoyed a broad range of activities that could also include being studious in the endless wonders of higher existence. Experiencing things they wished to do and further explore the marvelously infinite and awe-inspiring mind of the universe, is a godly pursuit.

Gods created their own assignments, which in turn became human realities. Assignments (jobs) could be administered and performed from wherever the gods happened to be. Gene manipulation and activation of mutations in animals, plants and insect species, are procedures propagated on planets and moons throughout the star system, by the gods. What differentiates superiority of the gods from humans was higher technological capabilities and an inside knowledge of things in the universe.

Gods brought to life any environment they wish to exist in, and not by illusionary Holodeck type realities, but by the technological authority at their disposal. Hyper robotics and bizarre whimsical beings, constructed physical environments for the gods, instantaneously or over time, by simple demands from the gods.

Star system gods are not omnipotent beings. But technological advantages give the gods super powers (paranormal abilities) that they use to rule over most of the inhabitants of their dominium. The gods call into existence any reality they chose for themselves, and occasionally, share bits of that reality with subordinate mortals.

Gods on assignments often wear bizarre headgear and body armor that is equipped with various gadgets attached or hovering near them. Such arsenals gave the gods invisibility and invincibility against most creatures and beings they confront.

Gadgets moved about the gods as electrons move within an atom. Most devices stir so rapidly that humans glimpsing the gods cannot see all the moving gadgetry or any of it, only the strange looking gods with bizarre headgear and body suits. Gadgets served various purposes and activated according to circumstance the gods found themselves in or put themselves into. Gadgets from the gods function with the intentions of the gods and sometimes independently of the gods, depending on the situations and the beings they interacted with or confronted. When gods come into contact with a number of humans or a single human, devices from the headgear descend on the human or humans, sterilizing and incapacitating the human(s) instantaneously. The bizarre gadgetry and devices prep minions for a visitation with the gods. Humans are rarely aware of such happenings taking place around them and mostly remember nothing about the encounter or that the gods visited with them. Many humans that are allowed to remember portions of the encounter are usually left horrified by the ordeal and believe they woke from a terrible nightmare.

Gods travel inside of ships but also travel accompanied only by their entourage of gadgets, without the need of a ship (UFO). Ships were used whenever humans or other types of cargo was transported, detained, annihilated or for the internment and processing of bodies and souls.

Stripping out souls from human and Martian bodies so that they could be placed into other types of beings, containers or places, for shipping and storage, is within the gods' prerogative and powers, while they are inside of specialized ships, and with the assistance provided by spiritualized beings. Spirit beings are only seen by the souls when allowed by the spirits and or during the time souls are being processed and moved outside of their bodies.

Gods come into existence from multiple sources; from souls moving up from utopian-classed planets and moons or are cherry-picked from planets and moons in this star system. Gods are not equal to each other and exist in strata of increasing privileges that allows access to higher awareness via the level of purity the soul has thus far attained.

After being admitted into the kingdom of the gods, gods continued to reach higher clarity and garner additional abilities (supernatural powers above and beyond gadgetry and physical matter). After the gods reach a certain level, they move to ever higher levels of existence and away from star systems altogether until they merge with the spiritual realm, from where few gods look back.

Advancing further away from the physical realms is a large step, and far more rewarding than escaping from the merry-go-round of the reincarnation cycle humans are stuck in. Escaping the physical dimensions of existence allows for rapid acceleration to absolute freedom, at levels that even the gods find difficult to grasp fully. The enormity of existence and the splendid inestimable array of things in the highest reaches of existence are astounding times a gazillion (no hyperbole).

Souls moving up from lower dimensions do not become gods of star systems until they have resided on utopian planets for specified periods and mastered the criteria for the job. Souls advancing from Earth-type planets spend brief periods in transitional realms, as spirits, before being placed back into physical bodies, and located on any number of utopian or pre-utopian planets existing in the galaxy.

Gods, as well as Serpents, Reptilians, and Renegades, set up shop on all the planets and cultivate, and then merge the offspring they birth with the native populations. Kings, emperors, and rulers (gods, Reptilians, and Renegades) were the higher beings that occasionally mixed their genetic material with selected humans. Humans on Earth, share similar genetic material but have dissimilar and distinctive racial qualities; qualities that are dependent on the lineage of higher or lower beings that originated the tribe that they came from.

HADES

Hades, or some such equivalent place, and there are many stages of horrific cosmic institutions, where mortals are stripped from their corpses and enter unwillingly, and naked, for all to see. Naked in the sense that souls wear their defects out in the open unable to hide their corruptions and flaws.

The underworld is filled with dungeons and mazes within mazes, created by individual souls. Each soul has their own mess of mazes to work through. There is no escaping the underworld for the souls placed into it until souls are released by the demons within each soul. The underworld resides inside the interiors of planets, moons and also on large container ships moving at great speeds on the fringes of star systems. Hades is an existence without sunlight, a dark, mysterious and frightful place, where souls linger in torments until destroyed or released.

Time is jumbled up in hades, where phantom souls wander while revisiting past lives and atrocities they figured into. Unable to change what they have done, souls agonize over the minute intricacies of pain and fear they helped create and perpetrated in a previous existence. Hades is a terminal nightmare those in it cannot wake up from.

Hades has endless strata where souls begin their long grueling journey that often leads to reincarnating back to the place they last died from. Depending on length and degree of crime the soul engaged in, while alive, how far down the strata they will find themselves; while in the loathsome quagmire. No food or water nourish the damned souls (yet they crave such comforts), while they travel through halls of mirrors that reflect the painful darkness within their own souls.

Dark worm-type creatures infest hades, tormenting and stealing away vestiges of tranquility that linger inside the souls of the damned. Terror and paranoia embrace empty souls who yearn for redemption, and a morsel of solace, where none exists. Even the escape through madness is deprived them who enter such places. Full awareness is a cruel punishment for those who would rather not know the pains they wreaked on others. The shame is overbearing, merciless and humbling, the latter if one is ever to escape the ruthless karma attached to them like a monstrous leech.

Souls accumulate at the top layers of Hades and are eager and desperate to reincarnate into any physical form they are allowed to incarnate into. Wild animals are the destination of many souls hungry for a chance to begin their trek anew, moving up and eventually into a spiritual path, as a soul fit for a mortal body. Desperate for redemption some souls are able to bypass animals and are given the opportunity to enter into mortal bodies in deplorable, war-ravaged lands, on various planets in the galaxy.

While at the upper reaches of hades, souls receive a deeper understanding of their circumstances and are allowed to grasp the options made available to them. After incarnating into mortal form, any clarification received by them, while in Hades, is taken away.

Souls subjected to entering wild animals retained some of their illumination that they received from Hades. The souls exist in a constant battle for survival against other animals while being feasted on by pestering insects and tormented by ever-present hunger and in the knowledge of why. Souls in the animal world roam alone or in packs and compete with each other for scraps of food until they die. Death brings no honor and souls are left with having learned nothing other than the depravity of existence in the cesspool that is at the lower levels of reality.

One level of hades consisted of people angered at the feebleness of mortality (horrified and annoyed that life goes on after death). Such souls loathe the fact that they are immortal and must pay for crimes committed by them. Souls roam disgusted with existence (admitting that had they known that life is forever, they would have acted differently). Tired of existence and yearning for everlasting peace (death), they continue to deny themselves opportunities to pursue and enjoy eternal life. Such souls linger longer in the underworld, choosing to haunt and torment other souls deep in the bowels of hades, where hate feeds eternally on all who indulge it.

A chamber of fractured horrors exists in the labyrinth of hades, where souls are splintered (split into more than one and less than many). Each part, like that of a shattered mirror, reflect on unique situations and perspectives that have taken place in their lives. The core of the shattered soul is kept in a locked chamber while its various parts incarnate into bodies of animals, insects and other kinds of beings (Martians), occasionally even humans. Should a sliver of the fractured soul be placed into a mortal body (or other such being), it can experience a normal life (rare), and even a pleasant life (rarer still). The sliver will not know about its schizophrenic multiple detachment states until it dies and returns back to the core soul.

A disturbing realization comes with the knowledge that it is a condemned creature in the pit of hell. And that the fractured soul will not be released until all its shattered parts return, and the soul is whole again.

The worse torment is to realize that life is enjoyable for infinite numbers of souls throughout the universe, and not be one of them. Having experienced a bit of that joy and knowing it truly is possible, makes it all the more agonizing when abruptly deprived of it. The more fractured the soul, the longer it will take before all the parts converge back into one. Many parts will reincarnate into other creatures or beings delaying and prolonging the anguish of the core soul. Some fragments of the soul will know and see the core soul in dreams while sleeping, or in memories that were left intact inside the mind of the creature. Slivers of souls that end up in animals or insects often have intact memories of their core soul, and agonize along with the core soul.

I asked to see a soul that was deserving of such horrific torment and endless punishment. Sam obliged and showed me a powerful man of Martian breed; who enjoyed watching humans and Martians fed alive to wild animals. A woman, who slowly poisoned her young, keeping them sick for the perversion of enjoying their torments. A soldier, pouring gasoline into the mouth of a wounded enemy combatant that was pleading for a drink of water.

Then Sam unloaded on me a visual that was highly disturbing, the acts of mortals against each other were atrocious and touched nearly every soul that has set foot on Earth, as far back as earth's early beginnings. All souls excepting for a few that land on Earth have soul issues that won't resolve easily.

Sam said that most humans don't see evil unless it is in other humans, seldom recognizing evil within themselves. Incarnations into the physical realms and torments between those realms are used by higher beings to showcase every aspect of the mortal soul, in its true black and white self.

INNER EARTH

Earth is small in comparison to other planets in the star system, and in the galaxy. Nevertheless, Earth is huge. Humans and the millions of animals, insects and plant life on the surface of Earth are significant, yet doesn't amount to much on the surface of the Earth. Oceans cover a large part of Earth's surface and hide within such large numbers of aquatic species that many will never be discovered.

Earth's interior is massive. Earth is not hollow, as some theories have suggested, but Earth has abundant caves and caverns, far below the surface and inaccessible to humans due to the crushing pressure at certain depths. At present, Earth's surface population is between 7 and 8 billion people. Insignificant compared to inner Earth's inhabitants, which is in the multiple billions. Some of the inhabitants are humans, most are humanoid or some other type of creature or being (intelligent or otherwise). Human technology will not detect the thousands of hidden population centers inside of the earth. Surface humans are routinely taken to inner-planet places during abductions and mostly returned unharmed, by their Alien captors. Black ops working for Alien beings do most of the initial handling of humans, turning over the humans to Grey Aliens or inner-earth beings for black operation purposes.

Earth had thousands of pyramid type structures covering large sections of the planet millions of years in the past. Most have been worn down by the elements of nature over the course of hundreds of thousands of years. Remnants of the vast network of structures exist in nearly every country, still, and hidden away under thick forests and mounds of dirt and thick strata of rock-shelves (that used to be part of the pyramids). In America, the Ozarks Mountains and the Appalachian Mountains, hide thousands of acres that once housed the huge pyramid structures that easily dwarf the ancient pyramids found around the world today. Structures that were designed to provide fortified shelter against monstrous creatures and beings from the stars that have rained down and invaded earth many times in the past, and will once again.

SOLAR BEINGS

Solar beings reside inside the stars (suns). They are spirit beings that command the whole of the physical star system yet seem indifferent to indigenous and foreign populations infesting the planets and moons spawned by the star. They are light beings, radiating energy with the same intensity of the star. The gods at the periphery of the star system say that the solar beings are the force behind the star, and an integral part of the star, but not the star. Solar beings are as a soul substance inhabiting a physical body, the star in this case. The star is not a physical body but creates elements of physical matter that incorporate the material orbiting the star.

Solar beings exist in numbers beyond reason and understanding by those not of their caliber, existing in a realm of their own and mostly unknown to the physical masses beneath them. Unlike other kinds of spirit beings that roam the physical and inter-dimensional heavens, solar beings seldom stray from their chosen star. As midwives, helping in the star's creation (after the star is born) and assisting the star throughout the star's longevity, up to the end of the star. Solar beings are then free to assist other new stars, in an endless ongoing cosmic cadence inside of every galaxy.

Light beings are not the originators of souls inhabiting humans and other beings within the star system but are made from the same nonphysical light-substance that exists behind and within matter, as do many types of souls. Matter and light have many mysterious connections and take on various forms inside and outside of dimensional systems and streams. Existing inside realities that have no alpha and omega (No beginning and no end).

Types of misunderstood matter, by Earth physicists, is the illusionary matter versus real matter. Real matter, a product of a sister dark dwarf sun, existed within a temporary sphere that has long ago slowly dispersed itself like a time capsule within the star system. Real matter impregnates illusionary matter, which is composed of elusive subatomic rhythms within atoms. Only shadows of real matter exist now, having distributed its elements into the whole of the star system eons ago. Such cosmic revolutions inherent in the light spectrum will continue without end.

Gravity is the product of matter and light (The twisting from one to the other and back). Matter is light, and light is matter, and the interaction between the two stages is gravity. As matter increases, gravity surges. As matter decreases (When nearing the speed of light), light surges (Matter turns into light), and gravity decreases.

The conundrum is that matter is in a constant state of moving at or above the speed of light (A conundrum for the 3D perspective). In essence, matter and light are one. What breaks the two apart (divides them), are the dimensional waves traveling through dimensions. Matter and light have far different properties the higher up the dimensional strata "it" travels.

Dimensions are infinite, and that puts a twist on the number of levels of spirit beings and the numerous variations of physical realities in existence.

Beings in the star system are not omnipotent, not even the solar beings within the sun. Supreme Beings reside elsewhere, and everywhere, and nowhere, in the enigma-rich embryonic lower dimensions, where wavering matter and wavering light, ring supreme in the rickety galaxies that fill this queer and enigmatic universe.

MANIFESTING DESIRES

Humans of Man manifested numerous inner desires within their span of life. All thinking beings fantasize about other realities, desires or deep needs to fill voids within their souls. Violence was not part of the many concepts humans of Man were aware of. Violence existed all around them in the star system and on many of the planets and moons humans visited and or lived on, yet humans were mentally blocked from seeing and knowing about violence. Instead, humans were free to fantasize and manifest pleasurable desires and making them into their realities.

Humans on Earth, manifest fantasies periodically, as a community in the form of festivities and holidays; creating temporary fun-filled realities with short duration periods lasting a few days or weeks at a time. Humans on Man individualized their fantasies, and their whole world changed into that fantasy until they fantasized another one. Fantasies lasted as long as the fantasizer desired it (while alive). Fantasies existed mostly in the mind, eliminating conflicting fantasies within families. When the whole family was on board with a fantasy, they could make it happen in their physical realm.

Modern humans have similar powers to make their bizarre fantasies into realities. Some humans can achieve their fantasies within their lifetime, most will not. But all humans will achieve their deep down desires in other lifetimes (If not in their current life), on other planets or places where such desires are prevalent and allowed.

Humans of Earth are enticed and then recruited by their desires. Humans that crave violence in one life are destined to live out that violence, if not in this life, certainly in the next life. Those craving harmony received likewise. Desires have a life of their own, and can easily deceive by masquerading evil and ego as strength and heroic qualities.

TRUTH IS DESPISED MORE SO THAN LIES

Lou Baldin

BOOKS BY THE AUTHOR

In League with a UFO........................1997

Shrouded Chronicles....................….......2000

A Day with an Extraterrestrial.............2008

An Italian Family...............................2011

Judas Crucified.................................2012

Orphans of Aquarius............................2012

UFOs in the Year of the Dragon.........2012

Mars and the lost planet Man............2014

Graduation into the Cosmos.............2016

Blog Chronicles (books) paperback and eBook (Kindle) format:

UFOs and Extraterrestrials are as real as the nose on your face...2011

Coming clean on Extraterrestrials and the UFO hidden agenda Part one..…..2011

Coming clean on UFOs & Extraterrestrials Part two....2012

Coming clean on UFOs & ET Part three ....…..2012

Coming clean on UFOs & ET Part four 2012

Coming clean on UFOs & ET Part five...................2013

Coming clean on UFOs & ET Part six.....................2013

Extraterrestrial Speak Part one.............................2015

Websites:

ufolou.com

baldin.proboards.com